Another Jekyll, Another Hyde

THE THIRD OF
ANOTHER SERIES

ANOTHER JEKYLL, ANOTHER HYDE

DANIEL & DINA NAYERI

CANDLEWICK PRESS

Copyright © 2012 by Daniel Nayeri and Dina Nayeri

The authors respectfully credit the original 1886 novel *Strange Case of Dr Jekyll and Mr Hyde* by Robert Louis Stevenson as reference and inspiration for this story.

First edition 2012

Library of Congress Cataloging-in-Publication Data is available.

Library of Congress Catalog Card Number pending

ISBN 978-0-7636-5261-6

11 12 13 14 15 16 SHD 10 9 8 7 6 5 4 3 2 1

Printed in Ann Arbor, MI, U.S.A.

This book was typeset in Slimbach.

Candlewick Press
99 Dover Street
Somerville, Massachusetts 02144

visit us at www.candlewick.com

"We should do Jekyll and Hyde for the last book."

"Mic check. Hello? Hello?"

"Yeah."

"Helllllooooooooo?"

"Yes, I'm here!"

"Cool. I had to get a sandwich, but I'm back. Jekyll and Hyde sounds good."

"Wow, OK . . . great. I didn't think you'd go for it so easily."

"Sure."

"It's just like you and me."

"Exactly!"

"I'm Jekyll and you're Hyde."

"Wait. . . . No. Hyde is the evil one, right?"

"Yes. I'm the good one. And you're evil and unpredictable."

"That's preposterous."

"No, it's what we just agreed. You're the Hyde of the family."

"I quit."

"See what I mean? Totally unpredictable."

To our editor, who deals with two Jekylls and two Hydes

PRISON

A two-faced moon hung over the black-and-white city, in turns shining as bold as the sun and hiding, shamed, behind the veil of cirrus clouds. The stars were either invisible or as obvious as pinpricks. Beside the city ran the Hudson River estuary, where fresh water crashed into the salty ocean and made a new mixture. The windows of the skyline alternated on and off. The people inside were sometimes both.

On the streets of the Upper East Side (where it was crowded and lonely at the same time), a mousy, unkempt school nurse scuttled across an avenue unnoticed. With one hand, she held a tissue in front of her mouth, to catch the occasional sickly cough. When a poodle barked at her, she shrank back, as though it might attack her. The owner of the poodle waved a casual apology and went back to his phone call. He couldn't have seen the hate in her right eye. Or the branded cross in her left.

As she turned the corner on a wealthy residential block, her stride began to steady, her posture to straighten. She looked to her left and right, then pulled the clips from her blond hair, which became more lustrous as it fell over her shoulders. The nurse ascended the stairs of a historical brownstone, and with each step, her form seemed to alter. Her indistinct features became more pronounced, elegant and classic. All except the burn of her left eye.

She swept past the vestibule and the mailbox that said FAUST RESIDENCE. The doors retreated as she approached. The viscous gloom within the house threatened to ooze out into the world. The space inside did not match the shape of the building from the outside. Through a silent hall, a center room appeared, and from there, a dozen other halls branched out, like the spokes of a torture wheel. In the central chamber, a wooden table sat heavily on dead legs. Above it, a chandelier made of a thousand tangled stalks held candles as varied in size and color as all the fingers in the world.

As she stepped into the center of the room, the nurse didn't seem to notice the two figures, standing with their backs pressed to the wall on either side of the entrance. The light of the candles flickered on their faces, both in a grimace, as though it was painful to exist in such a place. When the nurse reached the table, she began to peel away her jacket and said, "Children? Where are you, darlings?"

The two figures, one a boy and one a girl, stiffened in their hiding places. They had the rabid look of prisoners, victims of countless harms. The girl was squinting, either because of the swollen bruises on her cheeks or because she needed glasses. She held a shard of mirror like a knife, though it cut into her palm. If you listened very closely, you could hear the drops of blood drip onto the ground. The boy's blond curls were matted to his head with sweat and scabbing cuts. If he continued gnashing his teeth, the nurse would easily hear them.

She kept her back to the entrance as she continued to put on a long black dress. As soon as she lifted her arms and let the fabric fall over her face, the children sprang — not toward their nurse but away. They swung around the corner and sprinted, both of them limping, back toward the entrance of the house. The noise of their escape didn't bother the nurse.

The two ran, with bare feet, on a floor that seemed to break into jagged gravel with every step. The walls stretched to keep the exit from their reach, but finally, the girl collided with the door and began yanking on the doorknob. When the boy reached her, he tried to help, both of them frantic.

The voice of the nurse in the center room was calm, even pleasant, as she said, "How was your day?"

Finally, the door relented and swung open. Behind it was a brick wall. The girl was tempted to stab at it with her jagged shard of glass or smash into it with her shoulder, in the hope that she could crash through to the other side. But she knew there was no other side. There was no escape.

The boy turned and slunk back to the room. By then, the nurse had fully transformed into the beautiful governess she once was. Her blond hair was pinned up with a brooch the shape of a moth. "Hello, Madame Vileroy," said the boy, leaning on the wall. He winced and stepped away, as if the wall had pierced his shoulder.

"What was that, Valentin?"

"I mean . . . hello, *Mother*," said Valentin as he doubled over in pain.

The governess's gaze moved to the girl. "Victoria, come here and help." Begrudgingly, Victoria limped toward Madame Vileroy and held up the broken mirror, streaked with blood. Madame Vileroy looked into the mirror and pushed a stray hair behind her ear. With a pinkie, she perfected the outline of her lipstick. Victoria's arm shook with the exertion of holding the glass out straight, but she didn't dare bring it down.

Madame Vileroy straightened and patted down the creases of her dress. "There," she said. "Thank you, sweetheart." Victoria dropped the mirror and let her arm fall to her side in exhaustion.

"Now," said Madame Vileroy, "how was your day?"

Valentin couldn't hide his disgust. He was never very good at making stuff up.

"How was our day?" he said. "Are you joking?"

"Shut up, Valentin," Victoria warned. Even in their constant punishment, Victoria managed to keep a cool exterior, or at least a superior one.

"What do you want us to say?" said Valentin.

Madame Vileroy raised a bemused eyebrow. "You think I don't love you anymore?"

"Love us?" said Valentin. "We're prisoners."

Madame Vileroy turned and walked to a full-length mirror mounted on the wall between two hallways. She was already bored. Somehow, she had hoped Valentin could have come up with something better than the obvious. Ever since the other three children had escaped, the Faust family had had to contrive a plausible story for New York society. Currently, they were the envy of the Marlowe

School, taking a full year to study abroad in Geneva. All five over-achievers were conquering an international school—their exploits making it back to New York in the form of status updates and unverified gossip. High-altitude Olympic training in the Alps, Model UN, the runways of Milan—the five Faust kids were taking Europe by storm. It was as though New York hadn't measured up, the competition being just too easy, the pond too small.

But Valentin and Victoria had no idea where Christian, Belle, and Bicé had gone. And—they suspected—neither did Madame Vileroy.

She had only recently gained back some of her former self. Every day she scurried around Marlowe in the form of the nondescript nurse, playing some game with some professor's kids whom they'd never known and never thought worth knowing. Slowly, Vileroy was getting back her strength. And every night, she snuck home to check on her remaining children, trapped in the hellish house by their own cover story. They knew Madame Vileroy blamed them for the others' escape, or else their stay might have been remotely comfortable.

Instead, they spent every moment awake, tortured by the medieval horrors of the living prison—Victoria cursing the ones who escaped and Valentin cursing himself for not having joined them.

Madame Vileroy stared at herself in the mirror—just off perfection. She frowned and tried to figure out what it was. With two fingers, she pulled the skin at her temples. She turned to see her profile: left, then right. For now, she could keep the form for only a few hours a night, and she had to use her time well. While she searched for her lost darlings, she would need another story to tell the families of Marlowe. There was so much yet to do at the school. And so she was going on a date. But like Cinderella, she would need to run home before midnight.

Aside from a new mission here in New York, Madame Vileroy had more urgent worries. She had dallied in this vast metropolitan playground unchecked, because in the sleepless city, she was the one creature who was unencumbered by time. She had been immortal, but now time was running out for her, too, and she was forced to consider ancient provisions she had made for herself centuries before — the source of her immortality divided up into three distinct forms.

She would have to take inventory once more.

"So, after you seduce the widower, what will you say about us?" said Victoria.

"Nothing," said Madame Vileroy.

"You're never going to bring him here?"

"No."

"What happens when our 'year abroad' is over?" said Valentin.

"Figure it out, Valentin. The banker's just a temporary solution," said Victoria.

"That's right," said Madame Vileroy, finished with her inspection.

Madame Vileroy didn't seem bothered by the idea that her solution was temporary. To her, almost everything was. The only permanent concern was her lifeline, and that was something to which these children would never be privy. To them, she had the task of collecting souls. She would seduce the richest man at Marlowe, become a mother to his son, and, as always,

6

move along once the story was finished. She added, "And with all the plane crashes these days, maybe you won't need a way back from Switzerland. Maybe there won't ever be another Faust."

The thought occurred to both Valentin and Victoria at the same time, just as Madame Vileroy wrapped a sable fur coat around her exquisite form and glided down a random passage in the endless spokes of hallways. As she opened the door — this one a true exit — and bid her children good-bye, it occurred to them that they, too, might have been a temporary solution.

✳

WEDDING ANNOUNCEMENT

Charles Goodman-Brown, chief executive of one of New York's most respected financial institutions, and French governess Nicola Vileroy announced their engagement last week, after a short and well-hidden courtship. Details of the wedding have not been released to the media, though it is rumored that it will be the event of the season.

—C'est la Vie, NYC gossip blog

SOMETHING OLD, SOMETHING NEW

"You're Dr. Alma? OK . . . So do I just . . . talk for an hour?"

"Yes. You can talk about anything you like, Thomas. This is a safe space."

"Should I lie on the couch, or can you just shrink my head from over there?"

"Sit wherever you like."

"Because, you know, this wouldn't be the first time someone's poked around in my head. There was this crazy witch last year . . ."

"Why don't you tell me about it?"

"Never mind. You wouldn't believe me if I told you."

"OK, so tell me something I would believe. Your father says your girlfriend ran off to boarding school without saying good-bye. Tell me about this Belle."

"No, thanks."

"Thomas, might I make a suggestion?"

"I'm guessing you're going to whether I agree or not. I mean, that's why the Parents' Association hires ladies like you, right? To crack into our heads?"

"I may be employed by Marlowe, but I'm on your side, Thomas."

"That's rich. Even for this place. . . . You know, you look familiar. Have we met before?"

"No. Now, don't change the subject. Let me suggest this: if you don't want to talk to me, why don't you try keeping a journal? You can write in it privately. No one would read it. I think it would help."

"Whatever you say, Doc."

"A Halloween wedding? How gauche," said Mrs. Spencer as she plucked a single unruly hair out of her own head. She was sitting in the ballroom of New York's Four Seasons Hotel, straining to see the floral wedding arch from her seat in the thirtieth row. "Are those black roses? And what's the idea, sitting us all the way back here? She's learned nothing in her time here, Genevieve. Nothing!"

"The roses are crimson. And I think it's beautiful," said Mrs. Wirth — Mrs. Spencer's oblivious best friend and a lover of all social opportunities. "I love the fall."

"Charles looks scrumptious, though, doesn't he?" Mrs. Spencer sighed. Now that Charles Goodman-Brown, the most prominent banker in the city, was no longer a bachelor, there was little strategic reason to play coy. He was taken now; might as well salivate freely.

"What do you think she'll wear?" Mrs. Wirth asked as she

surveyed the room. It was midday, but thick curtains were drawn all around the ballroom to create a heavy darkness. Instead of sunlight, thousands of mismatched, misshapen candles lined the walls and crevices of the room, creating an illusion that the ballroom was on fire. Even the light fixtures above their heads had been replaced with four specially imported antique candle chandeliers. The effect was nothing short of spectacular. "She has wonderful taste," Mrs. Wirth droned on. And Mrs. Spencer had to admit, she would never have thought to mismatch the candles to mask the artificiality of it, or to challenge every fire code ordinance for the sake of ambiance, or to create an ancient feeling by blowing gentle streams of cold wind into the room, antiquing the chairs with rust, making the chandelier swing just slightly every few minutes as if it might be trying to run away . . . and what a clever idea, singeing the edges of the curtains. *Wait, were the curtains singed before?*

"If she pulls a Miss Havisham, comes out here all cobwebs and dust, I'm leaving," said Mrs. Spencer. "The woman is *bizarre.*"

"She won't," said Mrs. Wirth. "Trust me. She likes to get a reaction with this stuff, but I've never seen her looking anything but impeccable."

Across the room, Mrs. Wirth's son, Connor, sat with his lacrosse friends and pretended not to notice the spitballs hitting the back of his head courtesy of Marlowe's resident nerdling, John Darling. Connor's best friend, Thomas Goodman-Brown, was standing next to his father, the groom, under the crimson-flowered arch. Thomas's eyes were bloodshot, as usual, and he was fidgeting. He kept pulling at his bow tie as if it were choking him. A few drops of sweat dotted his hairline, and he wiped them away with his sleeve.

"I can't believe he didn't sober up for his dad's wedding," Connor muttered.

"I can," Wendy Darling said, and then turned to her brother. "Enough with the spitballs." Connor ignored her. He hadn't forgiven his ex-girlfriend for last month's incident with the resident adviser, even though Peter was fired and long gone.

"Fine," muttered John, and he went back to tweeting on his phone.

@SciFiClub @FutureCEOs @Page6News *Thomas baked at own dad's wedding. (Goodman-Brown shindig. Whatevs. I was invited ages ago) #MyAwesomeLife*

"Hah! 140 characters exactly on the first try! Suck it, psssh."

"John!" Wendy turned around again. *"Shut up!"*

"It's OK, Wendy." Connor sighed. Since last year, he knew less than anyone about his supposed best friend, Thomas, who was hanging out less and less with Connor and the other athletes and had begun going out to clubs, sometimes with the boarding-school kids, sometimes alone. Once in a while Thomas made time for Annie Longborn, who sparked some interest in him and seemed to be the only person who could summon the old Thomas back, even for a few seconds. If Connor asked her, Annie would tell him how Thomas was doing. But Connor didn't ask. Annie and her best friend, Roger, weren't in his circle of friends. And Connor didn't want anyone to know that Thomas barely had time for him anymore.

A boarding-school boy with white-blond cornrows, a fifth-year super-senior who was probably already twenty, leaned over and said, "Got a lighter?"

"You can't smoke here, stupid," said Connor.

"Why not?" said Cornrow. "The best man is as high as a bird over Amsterdam."

❧

Overwhelmed by eager guests, Charles Goodman-Brown didn't have time to notice his son's agitation, or his bloodshot eyes, or the fact that he seemed to have drowned (or smoked out) his sorrows by himself all morning long. In the months since Thomas's first real girlfriend had left, there were a lot of mornings when people couldn't say where Thomas was or why he had committed this reckless act or skipped out on that midterm exam. In just a few short months since last spring, Thomas had transformed into a sad, brooding creature. Though he wasn't so far gone that he didn't keep up a good charade. Thomas was still the most popular boy in school, still a debate team champion and future lawyer, and even now he was the quiet eye of a hurricane of high-school girls.

"He's just growing up," Mrs. Wirth liked to assure Thomas's father. "Just send him to the school counselor." But ever since Belle Faust moved to that boarding school in Switzerland, Thomas's "growing up" had taken a turn for the scary.

❧

The string quartet, featuring only cellos and basses, began to play an eerie version of Bach's *Sleepers, Awake!*

A gust of wind blew through the room. A few candles went out.

From the shadows in the back, a regal figure stood shrouded in silhouettes.

And then Nicola Vileroy, unaccompanied, unrepentant, began her slow procession toward Charles Goodman-Brown, her future husband. Maybe it would be more accurate to call him her *next* husband. None of the guests knew, because no one dared to ask anything about this woman's history. Had she been married? How many times? What had happened to the other men? Did she have children of her own? No one asked why the five orphans she had adopted were absent from the wedding. Yes, they had moved to Switzerland for boarding school, but could they not take a weekend off for such an important occasion? Did they not miss their surrogate mother?

As the beautiful governess walked down the aisle, no one thought these things. They were busy taking in all that surrounded them — all the old and the new — because unlike the aged fabrics, the amorphous piles of wax that were the candles, and the rusted chairs adorning the room in an old-world splendor, Madame Vileroy looked fresh and mesmerizing and in every way an incoming queen. She wore a long-sleeved dress made of ivory silk that elongated her figure and flared out like a mermaid's tail at her feet, then stretched and dragged behind her, gathering dust and insects with its heavy creep. She was a vision, not of a governess but of someone better. Someone a step above who answers to no one.

Not a wily governess nor a mousy nurse.

A stepmother.

—✂—

The trouble with having a stepson like Thomas was that he had experienced way too much of the uglier side of Madame Vileroy. He had been the victim of Victoria's Sunday dinner games. And he had watched Belle transform before his eyes at a school dance. Did he really see what he thought he saw? Did Belle become ugly? Did her face change and crumble onto itself like a wax doll? It's so easy to convince oneself that the mind is playing tricks. It's easier to question your own sanity than to give way to the supernatural — the devil, hellish faces, and other worlds.

Still, once a particular horror has been blamed on a mind trick, it is impossible to cover up a similar occurrence that way again. And that was the reason that, as she walked down the aisle and took Charles's hand, Nicola Vileroy was thinking of one thing only: how to put an end to the party. Because you can't pull off the same trick twice, and she could feel herself changing now. Even though she had her old body back, last spring's weaknesses were far from gone, her body struggling and then failing, so that soon she would be the plain-faced nurse again.

After the ceremony, the crowd adjourned to the lavish banquet hall, and Nicola Vileroy retreated to the bride's room, where the ancient governess doubled over and heaved. She looked up to examine her flawless face in the mirror — though not flawless any longer, because now she had a mark here, a blemish there.

She looked down at the train of her dress. Was it that long before? Or had her body shrunk just a tiny bit? She had only about an hour, and then she would have to retreat to her nightly solitude . . . it had come early tonight. Every night since regaining her beautiful body, she had shrunk back into the body of the nurse for a few hours of private recovery. Usually, this was the time she slept. But tonight she couldn't leave before her guests. She had to hide, since this was a ritual she couldn't avoid. Not yet.

Not to worry, she told herself. Very soon she would regain all her previous strength and the nurse would appear less and less, and then maybe never. Earlier in the fall, when she had not yet repaired the governess Vileroy, the school nurse had been the biggest part of her. At first twenty-three hours a day, then eighteen, then ten, as the beautiful French matron recovered at night. Then there had been the incident with the Darling children, and the nurse was beaten and no longer able to bear the brunt of the everyday. Luckily, by then Vileroy had recovered — her favorite character to play — and now . . . now she was almost finished with the nurse's tiresome face . . . though it still plagued her, sometimes appearing unexpectedly.

She slathered makeup onto her graying skin, pulled herself to her full height, and swept out of the bride's room. The reception was already in full swing and Madame Vileroy marveled at the guests' capacity for frivolity and waste. *Look at their foolish preening and pretend happiness.* After thousands of parties and balls and galas and coronations attended over the centuries, this old governess could almost hear each of the guests ticking things off lists. Even the ones who weren't here to suck up to the groom or finish off a business deal or win an invitation to Mrs. Wirth's Christmas party had their agendas. She eyed a middle-aged man in a cheap suit, sitting alone in a corner. He didn't belong here. He was probably here as someone's date, and he looked like he was worrying about a hundred small things.

Work is not everything. I will have fun like a normal person. Work is not everything. I will have fun like a normal person.

Madame Vileroy nodded to the man and plucked his name from among his thoughts. *Paulie.* She would keep this for later. Then she spotted her target. Thomas was sitting alone at an empty table, while his friends were gathered around the bar.

"Hello, Thomas," she said as she accepted a glass of champagne and sat in the chair beside her new stepson.

"Hi, Nicola," said Thomas. "Look, I'm thinking of taking off."

"Call me Mom."

"No," said Thomas. Madame Vileroy was not surprised at his response, since this wasn't the first time they had had this conversation. He got up and started to walk away.

"Leaving so soon?" Madame Vileroy asked.

"I'm tired."

From one side of the room, the photographer emerged and began snapping candid shots of Madame Vileroy and Thomas. From another side, a trio of women started to descend on the governess with their oohs and aahs about the wedding and her dress and her exquisite taste in cakes ("There is no food like devil's food!"). Madame Vileroy saw the middle-aged man watching her from his lonely corner. She made a show of ignoring the women to approach him. As she came closer, she saw him sitting up higher, looking around nervously as if he expected the bride to be approaching some invisible person sitting next to him.

"Hello, Paulie," she said, and took the seat beside him. *The police commissioner. That's handy.* "I'm so glad you could make it."

The man's watery eyes grew large, and he pointed to himself and said, "Me?"

Madame Vileroy laughed. "Who else? Look, darling, I have a

favor to ask of my favorite police commissioner. Though I really shouldn't make you work."

"Why not?" The man was looking eager now, and curious. He tried to make a joke. "Your other guests are working."

"I'm sorry?" she asked, pretending not to get the joke, because it is always good to make people feel inadequate and grateful.

"Um . . . my date," he said. "Never mind . . . I just meant that Cindy's networking with clients over there, so I have time. What can I do for you?"

Madame Vileroy glanced at the chattering redhead wearing a pantsuit to a wedding. "Lovely. Well, I know you're enjoying the party. People come to these things to have fun, after all." And then she laughed and touched his hand. "But since you're offering, I'm worried about my new stepson. I think he may be under the influence of the wrong sort. . . . I'm not sure. . . . I think some of his friends may have crashed the wedding . . . and maybe even carried in unsavory substances." She whispered the last part and looked at him with whimpering eyes. Did he see the broken left eye? Probably not. She had a way of displaying or hiding it according to her needs.

Commissioner Paulie practically jumped up from his chair. "Which one's your stepson?" he asked, and Vileroy smiled with genuine satisfaction — because this oblivious man was the only person at the party who didn't know exactly who was who. His world was made up of suspects and victims and perps, so much so that he apparently hadn't even noticed Thomas standing in front next to his father throughout the ceremony.

18

"That one," she said, and pointed to a circle of boys that now included Thomas, Connor, and an out-of-place John Darling. "The little one . . . the one with glasses." And then she pointed right at John Darling. "That's my Thomas. Please be discreet."

A few minutes later, Madame Vileroy was at her new husband's side, surrounded by acquaintances, hangers-on, and well-wishers. From the corner of her eye, she watched Commissioner Paulie in action.

First he stood a foot away from them, expertly scanning each teenager to see which one was most likely on drugs. Which one was fidgeting? Which one had red eyes?

She willed him to move faster. Already she could feel herself losing the battle to keep her body for a few more minutes.

In the middle of Mrs. Wirth's monologue about upcoming fund-raising activities at Marlowe, she began coughing uncontrollably.

"Are you OK, Nicola?" Mrs. Spencer asked.

She nodded and dabbed her lips, now just a bit thinner, with a napkin.

Commissioner Paulie had zeroed in on Thomas and was approaching the boys. He took care to place distance between Thomas *(the perp)* and John Darling *(the victim)*. Having recovered somewhat, Madame Vileroy smiled graciously at her guests.

The commissioner pulled Thomas aside. At first they talked quietly.

Then Thomas began gesticulating, and the commissioner grabbed his wrist.

Thomas shoved him away.

It took only a second for Paulie to pin Thomas's hands behind his back.

"Oh, my goodness," said Nicola as she pulled on Charles's tuxedo sleeve to distract him from his conversation with Mr. Wirth. "What's happening to Thomas?"

Charles looked up and immediately started to rush over to his son. By now, the whole room had grown hushed and everyone was watching. Before Charles could reach the commissioner, Paulie had pulled a small plastic bag of herbs out of Thomas's pocket.

"What in the hell is going on here?" Charles demanded. "Who are you?"

"Don't worry, sir," said Commissioner Paulie. "I'm taking this boy in. You just go on with your party."

"That is my son, you loon!" Charles roared. "Let him go right now!"

The commissioner looked baffled. His face went white, and he began to stammer. "But . . . but . . . she told me . . ."

A few snickers and disbelieving sighs drifted from the crowd of guests. The police commissioner's wife, Cindy, stood by, horrified, probably hoping that she hadn't introduced Paulie to anyone important. The commissioner was humiliated. From across the room, Nicola Vileroy challenged him with her eyes, daring him to see the truth. A blue and broken flash telling him that it didn't matter what these people thought. He collected himself and faced Charles. "I'm sorry, but I have to take him in," he said. Suddenly his job was everything to him. "I have to do my job."

With that, Thomas was dragged away.

Charles Goodman-Brown forced out a funny speech asking the

20

guests to stay and enjoy the party. He and his new wife made a quick and strategic exit — he to the police station, she to the warmth and privacy of her nightly bath, where she shut herself each night, avoiding Charles, communing only with the colonies of moths who, for a few nightly hours, were the only witnesses to the whereabouts of Marlowe's missing nurse.

THE PERP

Journal entry #1

Let's get this over with. I have to write at least four hundred words on "how I feel" for Dr. Alma. Well, Doctor, I feel fine. Or, to put it another way: the way that I feel, physically, emotionally, and most of all psychologically, is a state of being that would best be described as "fine." Thank you, Doctor, for asking. Now that I've expressed myself, I feel better than fine. Maybe even "fine and dandy."

That was only 76 words. This is brutal.

I guess I can talk about my mom. She had long sandy hair and a thin face, high cheekbones. She's been gone for years now. My dad says, "She is no longer with us," as though she ran off into the woods of Central Park and never showed her face again. I think he still can't say "died," even though the funeral was the summer before eighth grade. I remember random things, like a jingle she hummed all the time. A ruby bracelet she dropped down a sink. Our monkey-face tournaments. Dumb stuff.

The psychiatrist they gave me back then was a fat guy named Jeff. My dad buried himself in work. He's a business guy. He'd be on the phone and say something like, "Tell them we can't put it in the contract, but we'll move forward in good faith." And I'd jolt from whatever I was doing—my mom's name was Faith.

Jeff was useless. I'd come home and yell about his idiotic suggestions. ("Why don't you make a diorama of your mom's photos?" Yeah, no thanks, numb nuts. She's my dead mother, not my science fair project.) I'd always end up crying. Dad would listen, then we'd go up to the roof deck and throw paper planes off the side. If he was still at the office, I'd get online and he'd play an MMO with me. I bet he's the only CEO dad who plays as a Dwarf Fighter. We'd just run around and talk. We haven't done that in a long while. Our guild probably moved on.

How many words has it been? 352.

Apparently, I have depression issues just because Dad's marrying the governess of the girl who dumped me last year and then flew off to Geneva. And I've been getting these flashbacks of stuff that never happened. Belle crying. Victoria attacking me. Whatever. Six. Words. Left. 398. 399. 400.

✧ ✧ ✧

The holding cell was an empty cement cube, except for the camera in the corner of the ceiling, the wooden bench along one wall, and the billionaire's kid sitting on it. Thomas Goodman-Brown leaned on the wall, arms crossed. His tie and jacket were slung over the bench next to him. His collar was unbuttoned; his eyes were closed. He didn't move. After about an hour he realized that no matter what you do in an empty room, you end up looking crazy. Sane people don't hang out in empty rooms. It's about as unnatural as a Twinkie. There's no civilized way to be inside — if you sit and stare into space, you look like a cold-blooded killer; if you pace in circles, you're a meth head. If you lie down on the cement floor . . . well, nobody lies down on that floor. So they set up a camera to watch it all — the perfect evidence. Some junior officer might put it up on YouTube, and no matter what you're doing inside that vacant space, the comments will still say, *Holeeee Sheeeeeeets. That iz 1 crazy F&#k!*

That's what the camera was for — to make you look crazy.

Thomas alternated between leaning on a wall and pacing. He had so much energy that he was shaking. His wing tips made an aggressive clacking sound. Through the long vertical window in the metal door of his cell, he saw an officer walk by and he ran to the door. But the officer was already gone. He tried to look as far down the hall as he could through the reinforced glass. Nothing.

"It wasn't even my weed!" Thomas roared with frustration and slammed his palm against the metal door. Then he remembered the camera. He took a second to slow his breathing, the way he was taught to do just before hitting a golf ball. Then he crossed the empty room and sat on the bench. He didn't move for the next half hour.

His dad would be proud. If the old man ever showed up.

The door of the holding cell slammed open. Thomas looked up. An officer he hadn't seen before stepped to the side to let Connor Wirth and two men in gray suits enter the cell. The commissioner who had brought him in from the wedding was probably at home asleep right now. "First of all, I don't know why you took him to Washington Heights," said Connor as he tossed a handkerchief to Thomas. Thomas wiped the ink from his fingers and looked at the two men in business suits. Neither of them looked older than twenty-three. "Who are *they*?"

One of the men introduced himself, but Thomas immediately forgot the name. It felt strange to have Connor here. The two hadn't talked for a long time, and Thomas had the impression that Connor didn't approve of his new lifestyle. But now here he was, his best friend, bailing him out.

Connor looked over at the cop. "Can we go now, Officer . . . ?"

"*Detective* Mancuso," said the thin, prematurely graying officer.

"Oh, you got promoted, did you?" said Connor, with an awkward attempt at a laugh. Then he mumbled, "Um, good for you."

Detective Mancuso raised an eyebrow. "You paid the bill. You're free to go. There's just some paperwork in the front."

The two men, who Thomas now figured were lawyers, said something to Connor and followed Detective Mancuso outside to handle the last of the paperwork. Connor plopped down beside Thomas on the bench. "They look for real, huh? They're just junior assistants to some paralegal working for my dad's lawyer. No worries, though. You're in good hands." He settled back against the wall and took out his phone. "I've done this before," he said, and shrugged as if he considered it no big deal to get arrested. When Thomas chuckled,

Connor said, "What? You don't believe I'm street? You just wait."

Thomas tried to think of a way to thank his friend, whom he had shut out of his life for the past couple of months. It was easy to see that Connor was trying to seem badass for his sake — maybe he thought that's what it would take to be friends again.

Connor was silent for a minute. Then he took out a tin of Altoids and popped one into his mouth. "Those guys," he said, motioning toward the door where the lawyers had just left, "they're from a firm that could have OJ'd Jesus, if you get what I'm saying." Connor laughed at his own joke, which made Thomas feel better. Leave it to Connor to make a bad situation seem not so earth-shattering. "Let's get going."

Thomas handed back the handkerchief and grabbed his coat, and they walked out of the cell. "So," said Thomas, "since you've done this before, what comes next?"

Connor shrugged. "Well, I've *seen* it done before."

Thomas approached the processing desk and signed a few papers Detective Mancuso thrust in front of him, one by one.

"I'll admit," said Connor. "It did seem like a particularly one-sided episode of *Justice Makers*. But the congressman marched in there all lawyered up, demanded a bunch of stuff, and the weenie cop totally let his son go."

Detective Mancuso, who was still standing behind them, twirling his key ring, cleared his throat.

"I didn't mean you, Detective Mancuso. Ever watch that show? It's not bad. . . ." Connor's voice trailed off, and Thomas couldn't help but shake his head and snicker. The clerk handed him a plastic bag with his keys, wallet, and cell phone.

26

"No, son," said Detective Mancuso. He eyed Connor with a suspicious squint. "I don't really watch that show."

"You know, I don't even know why *I* watch it," mumbled Connor, his eyes on the floor. "I'm so busy doing my homework and, uh, giving of myself to . . . the poor . . . um . . ."

"Are you OK, son?" said Detective Mancuso, leaning in to check Connor's eyes.

Connor stepped back. "I'm just gonna wait outside. . . ."

Thomas followed Connor and the lawyers to the exit. "Thanks, again," he said to Connor as he pushed open the double doors. It was past midnight, chilly and clear. In the distance, Thomas could see the penthouse of the building where his father worked. The street was double-parked with squad cars. And still no sign of his dad.

"No problem," said Connor. His eyes looked a little glassy, and Thomas was about to ask if everything was all right when Connor started glancing around. Then, out of nowhere, he said, "You know what you should do? You gotta change all your status updates to: *Eff the po-leese.* Or: *Just got out of jail.* No! Call it *the clink.*"

"Yeah," said Thomas. "Hey, are you feeling OK?" Connor was usually pretty serious, never hyper or overexcited. Back when they hung out every day, Thomas used to joke that Connor did everything with the focus and gravity of a Navy SEAL. Now he was laughing it up, acting almost manic. But then again, Thomas wasn't one to judge, since he hadn't hung out with Connor in a couple of months. Maybe this was how he was nowadays. He had had his own girl problems.

"Thanks, guys," said Connor to the lawyers. "You can bill my parents."

"Hey, really sorry about the trouble," said Thomas. He was about to say again that it wasn't his weed, but figured, Why bother? He wondered if they would give him a lecture now, but they looked too young for that.

"First offense," said one of the men. "No big deal. You still have to show up to court, though. It'll probably just be community service."

They shook hands, and the lawyers hailed a taxi. Thomas and Connor started to walk away from the station to where Connor's driver had parked. Connor took some earbuds out of his pocket and popped one into his left ear, letting the other dangle at his side.

"You know what'd be a cool job?" he said, bobbing a little too vigorously to the music. "Hype man." He started beatboxing, but mostly it came out as spittle and machine-gun sounds. Was he on something? Nah, Connor was as straitlaced as they come. He'd never show up stoned to a police station — and he was just fine a minute ago while he was talking to the officer. Thomas glanced at his friend. His eyes weren't cloudy or unfocused or bloodshot. He showed none of the signs of any herb Thomas had ever tried.

"All right, here I go, here I go," rapped Connor in his tough-guy voice. He waved his hands as if he was mixing on an invisible turntable.

> "With that ink on mah fingers
> I'm a dead ringer —
> Either votin' in Baghdad
> Or got caught with a dime bag.

Guess I'm just a sad lad

Rebelling on my bad dad."

"Yeah, that's real good," said Thomas, trying not to look embarrassed for his friend. He wondered for the last time what had happened to his dad. As the cop pulled him out of the party, his dad had promised to come get him. Had he changed his mind? Was he teaching Thomas a lesson? At the wedding Thomas hadn't had enough time to explain himself. Sure, ever since Belle left — and even before that — Thomas had felt like he'd gone off the rails. At first, he figured he was just depressed over losing the first girl he'd ever been serious about. He couldn't focus on debate. His memories were clouded. Studying was impossible. Golf took too much attention. He'd even had a few minor blackouts. It was more than depression. He felt like someone had put a hand over a part of his mind — a black hole that ideas randomly fell into. People said things like, "You aren't feeling yourself today, are you?" Thomas was feeling himself, but just half of it.

Most people assumed he was taking drugs. At Marlowe, some kids had a dealer on retainer. Others flew to Amsterdam on the weekends.

Even his dad had approached him about "experimenting with substances." Sure, he had experimented, but he wasn't hooked on anything. Nobody believed him. They actually thought he was high at the wedding. He could tell by the way they looked at him, the way they judged his red eyes as a sure sign, when really he was just sleep deprived. And so, like any innocent person wrongly accused . . . he gave up trying to prove himself.

It was insulting, though. A pocket full of weed at his dad's wedding? Thomas was out of sorts, but he wasn't stupid. Besides, two hundred socialites in a penthouse is practically a coke den. How in the world had the officer homed in on Thomas? And how did the drugs get in his pocket? Did he misplace his jacket at some point? Thank God he had passed the urine test.

His dad's no-show shouldn't have surprised Thomas. It was a new era, after all. The man had a wife now. Maybe Nicola Vileroy was so interesting that Mr. Goodman-Brown forgot that his son was sitting in jail for no reason.

The two boys stood at the corner of two empty streets, scanning for the car—maybe the driver had pulled around for them. A few off-duty cabs passed by, heading home for the night. Connor flung an arm over Thomas's shoulder and started to hum, while Thomas smiled weakly and thought about how much he wanted to go home.

How had Connor become like this so quickly? His voice grew high-pitched, and he was talking really fast. Was he on speed? But how? He had been fine in the police station.

Connor leaned over, his nose an inch from Thomas's cheek, and tried to whisper (but really shouted), "Hey, Tommy, listen. I should probably tell you about my meds."

"No kidding," said Thomas. All this time, the two friends had stayed away from each other, supposedly because of Thomas's partying and Connor's perfect jock lifestyle. But now what was this?

"Want some?" said Connor. He laughed and put his finger up to his lips. "But, bro, you really can't tell anybody, OK? I got attention problems . . . I got swim meets . . . I got troubles, my friend, and this stuff's the happy trucker's choice!"

30

"Right," said Thomas. "So you took the meds . . . when, exactly?"

"I think Wendy broke my heart," said Connor. He pawed at his heart, as if he could grab a few pieces to show Thomas.

"I'm sorry about that," said Thomas, patting Connor on the back. He felt bad now, but what could he do? "We should find the car."

Connor reached into his pocket and pulled out the tin of Altoids. "Here."

"The Altoids box?" said Thomas. "Nice. Way to almost get us locked up."

"Dude, you . . . *were* . . . locked up!" said Connor, practically screeching with glee. "Besides, this is totally legal. I got a prescription for my ADHD."

Thomas shook his head. He felt sorry for his friend. Where was the car? Connor started texting someone on his phone. Thomas glanced at the harmless-looking box of mints in Connor's other hand, but before he could consider the idea of trying one, he heard a honk. A black car pulled up in front of them. "I had him park around the block," said Connor. "I didn't want cops to think we were rich kids. They might be prejudiced."

"So you swaggered in, wearing Paul Stuart, with two of your dad's law-school goons? Good thinking . . . throw 'em off the scent."

Connor fist-bumped the driver through the window. "You wanted me to wear a tracksuit to your dad's nuptials? That's uncouth." He jumped into the back of the car.

"Hey, Carlos," said Thomas. He sank into the leather seat, exhausted. If he could just get to his bed, he would sleep for the entire weekend. Maybe by the time he woke up, his dad would be divorced, Belle would be back from Geneva, and Connor—who was cycling between hyperdrive and a crash landing—would be clean and sane.

"Where to?" said Carlos.

Thomas said, "Home," just as Connor said, "Club Elixir."

As the car pulled around the corner, the two boys bickering in the back, neither of them noticed an SUV speeding toward the police station from the other side of the block. It came to a screeching halt. Mr. Goodman-Brown, still wearing his wedding clothes, jumped out and ran into the precinct to bail out his son.

THE ELIXIR OF WTF

"Tell me about your mother, Thomas."

"No. Why don't you tell me about your mother?"

"My mother was a Swedish nurse practitioner who died of breast cancer at the age of sixty-six. She left two children and a loving husband."

"You get asked that a lot, don't you?"

"You're not my first angry young man."

"I'm not angry."

"OK. What would you like to talk about instead? Your nightmares about Belle, perhaps?"

"I'm not angry. Not wanting my dad to marry some gold-digging fake French chick doesn't make me angry. Also, weren't governesses prostitutes at some point?"

"No. And it's quite a lot more than that, wouldn't you say? You've begun skipping school. Your golf coach says you've quit the team. And if I'm not mistaken, I smell alcohol on your breath. Did something happen with Belle?"

"You know, you talk just like her."

"Like whom?"

"Like my mom."

"Interesting."

"Wait. What is that?"

"I'm sorry, what?"

"That bracelet. You just put your arm up, and that bracelet—under your sleeve."

"It's just a ruby bracelet, Thomas. Can we get back to the subject?"

Connor grabbed two Red Bulls from the minibar. "You want something?"

"No, I want to go home. Carlos, could you please drop me off?"

"No, trust me," said Connor. "To the club, Carlos." Then he turned to Thomas. "You owe me. You've been MIA for months, hanging out with Annie and that Roger kid, not giving a damn about what's going on with your old friends. And now I bailed you out . . . Gimme my mints back."

Connor grabbed the "Altoids"—Adderall, Thomas guessed—and popped another one. He guzzled one of the Red Bulls to wash it down. Oddly, the Red Bull was what made Thomas start to worry for his friend. Connor was a star athlete . . . and not just for private school. He was actually Division I material in swimming and basketball. He hadn't had so much as a Pepsi in ten years. His body was like the engine of a Ferrari. And tonight, Connor seemed determined to cram nacho cheese into the gas tank.

"What are you doing?" Thomas said, bewildered.

"Look, Tommy," said Connor. "All my life—no, all our lives, you and me, Tommy, we've been good. We drink our vegetable smoothies. We thank the maid. We do sports, get A's, all of it. Geez, I knew how to use a friggin' oyster fork when I was five. And you know who ends up with Wendy? A criminal, that's who. A guy who calls her his *ho*. I should've kicked that guy's ass before he got fired."

They pulled up to a nightclub called Elixir, with a line wrapped around the block full of Jersey queens, reality star wannabes, and blog photogs. The bridge 'n' tunnel crowd. A no-neck bodyguard with a UFC haircut stood at the door. A few college girls laughed too loud and posed for the photographers.

"Connor, you gotta get over this," said Thomas. "I mean, I'm not really one to talk, but—"

"I'm not done," said Connor. The two got out of the car. The cameras flashed a thousand bulbs. "See this?" said Connor. "Time was, I wouldn't come to a club like this because of all the annoying heiress types that make everybody hate us. But why? Why be a good guy? Huh? Why be nice?"

Connor walked up to the bouncer. The crowd jeered. Connor and Thomas didn't look famous. They didn't even look twenty-one. The bouncer nodded and stood aside anyway, letting them cut the line.

"See that?" said Connor. "Why fight it?" He flipped off the crowd and walked into the club. Thomas followed, and the crowd booed as the door shut behind him.

The house music was a solid wall of sound. Connor walked straight to the VIP lounge in the back. As he passed the bartender, he pointed at the table and shouted, "Bottle of Jack." Then he grinned over his shoulder at Thomas. *"Lonely* trucker's choice."

He pushed past an out-of-place hipster couple. "I'm tired of losing, Tommy. She didn't even break up with me." The bartender said something to a nodding waitress. The club was packed with hip-hop stars, starlets, Russian mafia, and fashionistas. Thomas spotted three models waiting in the roped-off VIP section who looked vaguely familiar.

Connor grabbed a shot sitting on the table and downed it. He coughed. "Listen, Tommy. Tonight's on me, OK? I want you to forget everything about Wendy. . . . Just forget her and her thug boyfriend." Thomas didn't bother to correct him. Connor followed the three models to the dance floor. Thomas had no idea where Connor had met women like that. Were they escorts? Friends of his mother? It didn't really matter. A waitress came by holding a massive tray of liquor. "Where do you want it?" she asked.

Thomas shrugged. He wondered if he should dance. Is it lame to stand by yourself swaying to trance music? Do you just go up to these beautiful women and hope they don't laugh? He rolled one of Connor's mints between his fingers.

"Do you have one of those for me?" a voice said.

He turned to find a pouty-lipped girl around his age watching him expectantly. She was dressed in a black Lycra skirt so tight it could have been part of a catsuit and matching black platform boots that went all the way up to her midthigh. Her hair was as red as her lipstick. Her eyes were as blue as her eye shadow. And a sinful smile to match it all. She looked like a cartoon, as if she had tried too hard to fool the bouncers about her age.

36

"Excuse me?" said Thomas.

She leaned closer. "The *Addy*. Do you have one for me? I'm Nikki."

"Did Connor put you up to this?"

"Who's Connor?" said Nikki. The music was too loud for talking. Nikki eyed the dance floor, unable to keep her body from moving. Thomas looked at the Adderall pill, then at the girl. "You sure you want it?" He held out the pill in his palm.

She stared at him with narrowed eyes, as if she thought he was playing a game. After a moment she seemed to think that he was safe and said, "Yeah, those hardly do anything. I have something better." Thomas wasn't sure exactly where in the catsuit (or maybe a purse) she had been hiding the tiny glass bottle she now held out toward him. It was full of bright-red pills, like M&M's. They even had the white *M* stamped out on each one. She handed him the bottle.

"Are you serious?" Thomas laughed and uncorked the bottle. He let one slide onto his palm. "M&M's?"

"No," she said as she turned the pellet in his hand so that the *M* was upside down. "It's called W."

Thomas examined the pill, then sniffed it. It smelled sweet. Was this a joke?

The look on Nikki's face was excited, curious, like a kid being bad for the first time. She obviously wanted Thomas to be impressed by her bottle of stolen pills. Well, Thomas wasn't afraid of any stupid candy drug she might have found in her mother's medicine cabinet. Besides, this W couldn't be all that dangerous if an overeager girl with a sweet face like Nikki's was walking around with it.

"What's it do?" he asked nonchalantly as he swallowed one of the pills.

Nikki shrugged and slipped the entire bottle into his jacket pocket. "It's different for every person," she said, suddenly sounding much more certain of herself, more informed about the whole thing, than she had a minute ago. "You keep it," she shouted into his ear. Despite the pounding music and screaming clubbers, her voice sounded like a whisper. "And don't share any of it, OK? Promise not to share with anyone."

Thomas nodded, thinking what a strange request it was.

She repeated, "Not any of it."

"OK, OK," he said, wondering why he was even accepting the whole bottle. He didn't care. Already he was feeling like a rock star. The pill was sweet. Thomas could feel the room sway. He was dizzy. The noise started to feel like waves. His eyes began to blur. All he could see was this fantasy girl.

She pulled him toward the dance floor. The DJ switched the track. It was almost all bass. A beat that went *boom boom boom*. It got in his chest. It got in his hips. The girl in black Lycra must have felt it, too. Nikki. Her name was Nikki. She moved to the pulsating rhythm. It slithered up her body. The lights were thrumming and all Thomas could think was *boom boom boom*. Her hair was on fire — yellow now, like Belle's.

The music became harsh, irritating. A low whine grew louder and louder to a piercing high note. The DJ scratched the disc. Nikki was smiling at him. Then her smile became a sneer. She was Victoria. Why was she Victoria?

Thomas's thoughts flashed back to the night at the Faust home. Belle had invited him. He was prostrate on the couch. Had he forgotten this part? He was prostrate on the couch, and Victoria was hovering over him. She was doing something to his brain. She was looking into him, into his mind, and it felt like she was chiseling deeper and deeper. She was boring like a drill into his brain. Thomas could hear Belle screaming, "No!" Madame Vileroy was there, too. She was enjoying it. All he could feel was the pain.

In another flash, Thomas was back in the club. Nikki was gone. He spun around, but she wasn't there. His legs began to wobble. His vision went black. He fell down. The music finally stopped.

When Thomas woke up, he was back in Connor's car. His clothes were damp with sweat. All he could muster was a low groan. Carlos looked at him through the rearview mirror. "It's all right, T. I'm taking you home." Thomas made a noise to say thanks. He was going in and out of consciousness. He couldn't tell if it was all another hallucination. Soon they were back on the Upper East Side.

Thomas rested his head on the window. When he opened his eyes the last time, he noticed that they were close to Belle's old apartment. It had been sold a long time ago, and Madame Vileroy had moved in with the Goodman-Browns. But as they passed by, Thomas saw something that made him sit up. He turned to get a better look through the rear window. If he didn't know better, he could have sworn he had seen his new stepmother, looking a little shorter, a little worse for the wear, walking into her old apartment building, hurriedly, as if running from some unexpected embarrassment, with just a glance over her shoulder.

That night, Thomas dreamed of Belle again. Usually he dreamed of their first date or this one random moment in the halls of Marlowe. It was passing period; everybody was rushing around. Thomas was walking to biology when he caught a glimpse of Belle, but he couldn't push through the crowd to get to her. And right then, as if she'd sensed his presence, she turned and looked at him. Just before the mess of people crashed back into the scene, she smiled. He dreamed of that half second more than anything else.

Sometimes he dreamed of the future, when he would see her again. But that night, Thomas saw the dinner at the Faust residence — the night that changed everything between him and Belle. All he remembered was a wonderful evening with the Faust family. They were all as generically charming as a sitcom. But after that night, Belle suddenly became cold. They still went out, but she was distant. She always seemed to be thinking of something else, something she wasn't allowed to share. Thomas couldn't deny that he had changed as well. He couldn't put his finger on it. The night had become a traumatic memory that he had suppressed.

In the dream, the memory was perfectly clear for the first time. Images of laughter morphed into scenes of horror.

He was sitting on the couch, Victoria and Valentin goading him. Then Madame Vileroy lunged at him, and her face was twisted like a gargoyle's. Her black coat flapped like wings.

Then he was lying on the couch, unable to move. Victoria was scraping around in his brain, and some part of him could still feel it — like a patient waking in the middle of surgery. He was paralyzed. His mind was slowly ripping.

<div align="center">~~~</div>

Thomas sat up in his bed. The searing light of morning burned his eyes. A wave of nausea. His head spun. He was panting, or dry heaving—he couldn't tell. He put his face in his hands and suppressed a sob. Were the scenes that he saw part of a nightmare or another hallucination? *How long does W stay in your system?*

Thomas had never taken an unknown party drug like W before. *Was it always like this?* He felt like a dozen people had spit in his mouth. His eyes ached to the beat of his heart. His ears were still ringing. He had no idea what he had done or who he'd done it with. He needed to find Connor, who was probably passed out in some gutter. As bad as Thomas was last night, Connor had completely gone off the map. It took all of Thomas's strength not to lie back down. He pushed the blanket aside. He was still wearing the tux from the wedding. He smelled his shirt. Bad idea. It smelled like sweat, perfume, booze, and five kinds of smoke.

His bedroom door opened. The sound of heels on the wood floor was uncomfortably loud. "Good morning, Thomas," said Madame Vileroy. Thomas flinched at the sight of her. The image from his nightmare, of her twisted face, was still fresh.

Thomas moaned. "Good morning, Nicola." He tried to swallow, but his throat was dry. She was wearing a simple blue dress, holding a glass of fruit smoothie. Her blond hair was pulled up. She crossed the room. The *clack clack clack* of her heels felt like a nail hammering into his temples.

"Did you sleep well?" she said. Thomas didn't answer. *Was she always so cloying?* She sat beside him on the bed.

"I thought you two were flying to some island this morning."

"With everything that happened," said Madame Vileroy, "your father thought it might be best to postpone the honeymoon."

"Oh, suddenly the old man cares that I went to jail? Where the hell was he last night?"

Madame Vileroy clicked her tongue: *tsk-tsk*. Thomas risked opening his eyes and caught her reproachful look. "That isn't appropriate language, now, is it?"

Was she playing the 1950s mom just to piss him off? She had become his stepmom about twelve hours ago. Could she at least ease into it a little?

"Is that for me?" said Thomas, and she handed him the smoothie.

"Your father wanted to rush right out to get you," said Madame Vileroy. "I told him it would be best to wait a bit . . . to let you think things over." She smiled at him. It resembled a sneer. Suddenly, the motherly tone had been replaced with a matter-of-fact governess. "He listens to my advice, you know. It's very important that you understand just how inseparable we are."

Thomas wished he could stand so he could run out, but Nicola continued. "Your father and I are married now, Thomas. But you, you seem . . . split about the idea. Did you have a nightmare about Belle again?"

Thomas decided to risk it. He got up. He never really reached a standing position. His legs gave out before he could put any weight on them. The smoothie spilled onto his shirt. Thomas cursed and fell back on the bed, sitting up this time, with his back against the headboard. Madame Vileroy seemed amused.

Finally, Thomas caught his breath. He looked Nicola in the eyes and asked, "What did you do to me that night?"

He expected her to say, *What night?* or at least pretend to be caught off guard. Instead, her quartered left blue eye seemed to twinkle — a knowing wink. Was he still feeling the symptoms of the W? For a second, her face was as twisted as his new memories.

"I think you know what happened, Thomas." As she spoke, Thomas felt the breath leaving him, because even before she could finish, he knew that she was admitting to it all. "Belle betrayed you that night. She didn't want you anymore. It just took you much longer to understand."

That was a lie. It had to be. Thomas closed his eyes. Nicola's face was still there. He couldn't escape her. He wished he could sit under a scalding shower for a long, long time. "Go away," he said.

Footsteps came up the stairs and across the hallway toward Thomas's bedroom. Mr. Goodman-Brown's voice preceded him. "Honey, are you in here? Oh, Thomas, you're awake." True to form, Charles Goodman-Brown was dressed in a three-piece suit, even on the morning after his wedding. He was holding a fruit smoothie. It was the exact same color as the one on Thomas's shirt.

"Good morning, darling," said Nicola as she got up from the bed and walked across the room to kiss her new husband.

Mr. Goodman-Brown said, "I brought your favorite breakfast."

"Thanks," said Thomas, trying for a cautious tone. "So did Nicola."

"Isn't she great?" said Mr. Goodman-Brown.

"Yeah," said Thomas. "She's a dream."

Thomas couldn't stomach any more. He took another stab at

standing up. This time, his legs did their job. As Thomas held on to a dresser to let the dizziness pass, his father said, "You want to tell me what happened last night?"

"Yeah, I got carted off to jail for something I didn't do, and you decided to stick around here with your latest piece of social climbing a—"

"Thomas!" roared Mr. Goodman-Brown.

"What?" said Thomas. "You're mad I broke curfew? Who *is* this person in our house? How long have you even known her? Do you have any idea who she is?"

"She's your new stepmother," said Mr. Goodman-Brown. *That was a low blow,* thought Thomas.

"No, she isn't. And don't ever say that again," he said. "Have we forgotten that she shipped off her own kids to Switzerland? Did you even know that she attacked me at her house? She's a liar."

His dad peered at him in disbelief. "Thomas, are you still drunk?"

"Just ask her," said Thomas. "She drugged me or something."

"I don't think you need her help for that!" said his father.

Thomas stormed toward the door, but his dad grabbed him by the arm. They had never been in a physical fight before. Thomas tried to wrench his arm away, but his dad tightened his grip. Thomas winced. For a second, he saw his dad's glare soften.

"Thomas, you smell like an opium den. What do you expect me to think?"

Thomas sighed. His dad would never believe him. He didn't even believe that the drugs in his tux jacket weren't his. Why should he?

"Apologize to Nicola . . . now," said his father.

And if he wouldn't believe Thomas about the drugs, he would never believe that his new wife had attacked Thomas that night — so long ago, it seemed. Thomas glanced at Nicola, who was watching him over his dad's shoulder. She had won.

"I'm sorry," Thomas said, and pulled away again.

His dad loosened his grip. He whispered, "We'll talk about it later. Maybe when we meet the rest of the family."

"What are you talking about?" said Thomas.

"Oh, we meant to tell you earlier, darling," said Nicola. "But with all the fuss around the wedding . . . Anyway, it's time for you to meet my son. Your new brother."

Thomas touched his temple again. "I've met them already —" he said reluctantly, thinking of Valentin and Christian, whom he had befriended last year.

"Oh, no, dear," said Nicola, her voice calm even as she delivered the final blow. "I don't mean the children in my care. I mean my *natural* son."

"I . . ." Thomas squinted at his father, who nodded as though he already knew. Instinctively Thomas put his hands in his pockets, as if the answer could be found there. Nikki's bottle of W rolled into his palm like a cylinder of ice. He clutched it, momentarily surging with an addict's panic for his low supply. Then he let it drop again.

"He's around your age," said Mr. Goodman-Brown. "His name is Edward . . . Edward Vileroy."

"Not Vileroy," said Nicola in her pretty French accent. "He prefers Hyde."

4

ANNIE AND BELLE

Journal entry #9

A son? She has a son and she didn't tell us, and some-how I'm the only one who thinks this is suspicious. Dad doesn't listen to anything I say anymore, and OK, maybe I deserve it a little after last night. But look, I have things under control . . . no failed classes, no missed debate rounds. I'm handling it. Doesn't he see that? He should know that I wouldn't lie about the important stuff. Maybe I lied once or twice about going out or things I did, but does he really think I'd make up some garbage to try to ruin his marriage? Shows how much he pays attention around here. I don't know—maybe I'm losing it. . . . How do you tell if you have something rattling around up in your brain? Do crazy people know they're crazy? The school shrink must think I am, or she wouldn't make me come in once a week. She's worried about the nightmares. I saw her notes. After I

told her about the one with Belle's face melting and chang-
ing into someone else's, she wrote down, "Worrisome and
bizarre." She thought I didn't see. . . . I guess I can't show
her this entry now. . . . I'll have to do another one tomorrow.

But I swear on every sacrament—or whatever you're
supposed to swear on—that last night, all that stuff with
Nicola was real. When I told her about my memories of the
night with Belle and Victoria back at their apartment, she
knew what I was talking about. She admitted that I wasn't
dreaming.

I can't sleep. I may be crazy, but Nicola's something
worse. Wish I could prove it.

✧　✧　✧

In the morning, Thomas pushed through the Marlowe hallways, forcing his legs to take every excruciating step. He could feel his knees
bending, his thighs stretching, all the individual pores in his skin.
Every bone in his feet felt like an anchor weighing him down. OK,
maybe it was stupid to take a random party pill he'd never heard
of before. It didn't even come up on Google. He tried to pick up his
pace, to seem natural, but he had a feeling that his gait was suspi-
ciously slow—a ragged, bloodshot kid walking through what felt
like a roomful of mashed potatoes.

He already knew that he would try W again.

He didn't bother to think too much about beautiful Nikki and
her catsuit, or why she had given him the entire bottle. The one
or two times her voice rang in his ear, urging him not to share the
pills, he shuddered with the bizarreness of it and tried to think of

something else — the wonderful, powerful, exhilarating feeling of the red pills.

He decided to skip first period and find Cornrow and the other boarding-school boys. Connor would be in class. No use trying to find him — Connor Wirth would go to class in a body cast if it meant being eligible to play in a game. So the boarding-school kids would have to do for some distraction. A few weeks ago, Thomas would have felt guilty hanging out with them, since their leader, the RA, had stolen Connor's girl. But that guy was fired now, and Thomas liked Cornrow. The boarding boys usually didn't show up for early morning classes. It was a luxury of living on campus. They could show up for before-school required assemblies or detention or whatever else was too conspicuous to miss, then go back and sleep through first hour and show up unrepentant and unshowered for second or third period. Thomas thought that maybe he should move to campus. But he knew his dad would never go for it.

He had just pushed through the double doors when he heard someone calling his name. *Not today,* he thought, *please, not today.* It was Annie Longborn. He usually just avoided her on his bad days. Thomas wasn't dating Annie. But Annie was definitely dating Thomas.

"What's up, Annie?" he said, and didn't wait for her to respond. "Listen, I have class." Then he turned toward the door leading out to the grounds. He was usually good at hiding the aftereffects of his partying, but today, after the W, he didn't think he could pull it off. He ignored the mock whispers of Annie's best friend, Roger.

"I told you he's stoned or drunk again," Roger breathed. He adjusted his square frames self-consciously on his skinny face, just below that two-hundred-dollar wool hat he always wore to school, even on warm days. The guy was a fidgeter and a world-class gossip. Plus, Thomas was pretty sure he was after Annie, despite the fact that they were best friends. It was that whole romantic comedy routine — wake up, ladies, your misfit best friend hit puberty, looked to his left, and fell in love. Roger clearly hated Thomas.

"Thomas," Annie called after him, her voice closer now. He stopped and turned because it would be rude to ignore her. She had her long brown hair in a loose bun today, like the kind you see on sexy cartoon librarians right before they pull two pencils out of it and it all tumbles down. Annie's hair pencils were the special art-school kind for sketching. She was pale, skinny, and short, but so full of energy that she was sometimes a little scary — like a teeny-tiny, hands-on-hips enforcer of justice. She stepped closer, as if she was inspecting him. She hadn't washed her hair — he could tell by the smell of old hair spray and sleep, which he liked. She had probably been up all night helping with her mother's handbag website or updating her blog with illustrations and designs, which, he had to admit, were very good. None of her mother's thousands of loyal customers would guess that a teenager was behind the amazing interactive handbag *über*-site.

Now the hair spray was making him dizzy. Was it the W that was making his sense of smell so strong? That morning he thought he could smell the neighbor's breakfast. Was he dreaming? Now Annie was smiling her big, toothy smile, trying to cover her worry. "I called you last night."

"Oh, yeah," he said. "I was busy."

"What were you doing?" She looked hurt. He hated it when she looked hurt, because the guilt always caused him to take inventory of everything he had said. But he was too tired to think of a good lie just now.

"Went out with Connor," he said, remembering Nikki and feeling a whole new kind of guilt—though, to be fair, Annie wasn't technically his girlfriend. "New club."

The last time he had gone out with Annie and a reluctant Roger, Thomas had promised to show Annie around the city. Her family wasn't from New York. They'd moved to town from Minnesota a few years ago, and she had never really gotten to know the city like a native. She wasn't the type to dig around for dives and hidden back rooms. She still liked going to Times Square and the rink in Central Park. She read *Zagat*'s and had been to the Statue of Liberty twice. When he was dating Belle, he used to joke about taking her to see the Statue of Liberty. The old Thomas would have done that on a date, just to make the girl happy. But now he thought it was lame . . . automatic disqualification from being a true New Yorker. Last time they hung out, he told Annie he would take her clubbing one night—on a date. They had never had a real date. . . . Roger was always hanging around or meeting up with them halfway.

"Hey, look," said Thomas, reading the disappointment in Annie's face. "It was a guy's night. Some grimy place. Nothing you'd like."

"How do you know I wouldn't like it?" she mumbled.

Thomas glanced over at Roger, who was looking uncomfortable and smug, as always. "Hey, bud," he said over Annie's shoulder. Roger moved his hand once, in a short, stiff wave, as if he was wiping a windshield. There was a tight little smile on his lips that told Thomas that Roger was afraid of him and that he hated being the third wheel all the time. Somehow, this made Thomas like him a little. "You should have come out with us, Rog," he said, trying to bring back his old charming self—the Thomas Goodman-Brown that everyone loved. "Next time."

"Yeah, next time." Roger smiled for half a second. "I was gonna go to this new place tonight . . ." He trailed off, probably realizing that Thomas didn't care.

As he was about to make another excuse and leave, Thomas saw his debate coach approaching. This was turning out to be one crap morning. In the old days, a lot of teachers would have stopped to talk to him. He wouldn't have minded. He was popular with the staff. That was the old days—before Belle left, before that dinner from hell at her apartment . . . before the nightmares.

"Thomas," said the coach, scratching his salt-and-pepper side-burns and looking at some papers in his hand. "I wanted to talk to you about—hey, you don't look well," he said. "Maybe you should go to the school nurse."

"Yeah, I'll do that," said Thomas.

"Come to think of it," said the coach as he glanced down the hall, "you can't do that. The school nurse seems to have disappeared. Probably got sick of the job. . . . Maybe you should go home."

"Maybe," Thomas said, and started to walk away.

"Before you go," said the coach, waving his stack of papers in front of Thomas. "This evidence you found is all wack. I can't make any sense of it." *Wack?* Did the guy think he sounded cool? Thomas wondered how old the coach was. Thirty-five? Forty-five?

"Sorry, Coach," Thomas said. "I'll take care of it." He took the papers. Then he turned back to Roger and Annie and said something about lunch, just to get the coach to realize that their conversation was over. Thomas watched his teacher walk away and wondered why everyone wanted a piece of him. Maybe he had given them all a little too much in the past few years. Maybe that's why they all thought they owned him. Still, Thomas was too smart to just say "Screw it" to people. Success at Marlowe was the only way his dad would stay off his back.

"Great!" said Annie.

Thomas snapped back to the present. "Huh?"

"About lunch," said Annie. "Sounds great."

Thomas rubbed his bloodshot eyes. This was another weird thing that kept happening since last night. He would get distracted by one thing — like the coach just now — and do and say things that he would immediately forget, as if something outside his own brain was in control for those few seconds. What had he told Annie about lunch? This W was insane — different from anything he'd ever tried. He wondered who made it, where he could get more when his bottle ran out, and when. Did he have Nikki's number?

"I . . ." Thomas stammered, trying to remember.

"I told you," said Roger. "He's *on* something."

"Back off, Roger!" Thomas snapped. A few kids turned. Roger took a step back. It was really time to go now. "Sorry, Annie," Thomas blurted out, avoiding her gaze. "I'm busy all day. I don't know why I said that." When she didn't respond, he added, "I'll give you a ride home in my dad's car, OK? Just wait in front of the school at three thirty."

A dark look passed over her face, the kind of accusing look that he had seen only on adults. Belle never looked at him like that. He was always happy around her. Suddenly, Thomas just wanted to get away. He staggered off. He forced his way through the thick crowd of classmates — some of them saying his name or trying to get his attention in other ways — through the double doors, out into the sunshine.

Cornrow wasn't in his dorm room. Thomas knocked a dozen or so times and then slumped down next to his door. He would rest here for a moment. He remembered coming home from Elixir, seeing his new stepmother entering her old apartment, looking a little ragged. He had no idea why the memory suddenly came back to him, but it made him shiver all over. Then he thought about Nicola's new son and the missing Faust children. He tried hard to remember that night last year at the Faust home when he went to dinner with Belle. It was a Sunday. What happened to him there? He had flashes of memory that didn't fit into the picture. At first, after coming home that night, he thought the evening had gone perfectly. Good food. The kind of boring conversation you have with parents. He had liked Nicola then. But lately, images would flash into his head that didn't fit anything he had previously believed. The memories came out of nowhere, on their own.

Belle and Victoria shouting at each other.

Nicola standing off to the side, with her creepy other son, drinking red wine. Whispering.

People touching him.

Someone dropping a vase.

His head hurting, his body paralyzed.

Scrambling of moments, overlapping seconds, like botched-up film reels.

Stop! Something inside him lurched. He sat up with a start and noticed a patch of moths hovering near the door. He crushed one with his palm, and the others started flying around frantically, as if they knew what was coming. One of them flew right into the front pocket of his jacket, as if it were leading the way to something. Thomas reached in to pull it out. He scooped the contents of his pocket in one swift fistful.

A dead moth. His keys. An old penny. The cold glass jar from last night.

He held it up in front of his face. . . . *What a little bottle,* he thought, and yet it was quickly becoming his favorite possession. The red pills inside were shiny, like jewels held in sunlight. He wondered if Connor or Cornrow or any of his friends knew about W. How rare a drug was it? Where did Nikki find it? For now, he would keep it his own secret, since he had only this one small bottle of it. And besides, Nikki had said not to share. She must have meant that it was very illegal or expensive or hard to get. For all he knew, it could be the only small bottle of W in the whole city. Weird.

To be fair, it wasn't *so* surprising that she had given him such a big gift. Upper East Side girls were always giving him things and pretending it was nothing. It was their way of showing they weren't interested in his father's money. Little did they know that the gift givers were the ones he always avoided. Neither Belle nor Annie had ever even thought to give him anything, which made him believe that they weren't secretly plotting a takeover.

Tired of thinking about Nikki and his stepmother and the other mysteries surrounding last night, he popped off the cork and tossed one of the pills into his mouth. He swallowed hard.

He reached over his head and banged his fist against the dorm-room door again. "Let me in!" he shouted. After about three minutes, a groggy kid with blond cornrows, wearing a Tupac shirt over Brooks Brothers pajama bottoms, opened the door and said, "Dude, someone better be dead or I'm pulling teeth."

When he saw Thomas slumped by his door, he motioned him in. "You look *messed* up. You can't come to school like that, bro."

Thomas shrugged. He tried to get up, but couldn't lift himself. He felt half asleep, and the spot next to the door was starting to feel really comfortable. He thought about how different this was from last night's pill, which was a whole lot nicer. Why were the two different? It was as if the bottle were its own person and each pill was one of its emotions. Last night was excitement. Today was a slumped-by-the-door blues. When he didn't move, Cornrow reached down and grabbed the crook of his arm. He yanked Thomas's arm hard, so that he tumbled into the room. Thomas considered telling him about the nightmares, the flashes of memory. Maybe he had a cure for it. But all he managed to get out was something about hiding his bottle. Suddenly, a part of him was very aware of the need to make Cornrow believe that he was OK. At the same time, another part of him was exhausted and slowly falling asleep.

Cornrow said something. Thomas couldn't tell what.

Now Cornrow was just moving his lips, and Thomas worried that he would see him falling into a trance. He didn't want to look out of control.

But he didn't fall. Cornrow laughed as if Thomas had said something funny.

Did I say something funny? Did I say anything at all?

Then he felt himself nodding and heard himself replying to Cornrow. Again he had no idea what he said.

After that, there was just a series of bizarre half moments.

Cornrow laughing again. Pulling out his phone. Texting.

Thomas in the back of his father's car, vaguely remembering a promise to Annie.

Annie's number flashing twice across the screen of his phone.

Back in his room. Tossing his school uniform violently out onto the balcony. Hair gel. Cologne. Slipping into his favorite old jeans.

A flutter of red hair, like fire, then blond hair, somewhere in his room. *Belle?*

Then total blackness.

5

ROGER'S NIGHT OUT

"Thomas, are you listening to me?"

"Yeah, yeah. Sorry. You were saying it's all natural . . . the stuff with dad and his new wife. I already know all this."

"Tell me more about these dreams . . . about the night with your friend Belle."

"They're not dreams."

"What are they, then?"

"I think maybe memories. I keep remembering weird things. Being dragged around. Being hurt. Like someone torturing me."

"Thomas, you do realize that's preposterous, don't you? You must be careful not to let that night become an obsession."

"I'm not crazy."

"No one said that you were. You are just missing your friend, I think. Maybe you don't know how to handle the fact that she is gone, and it doesn't help that you now share a mother . . . er . . . stepmother. Brings back old memories. But what about this new girl . . . Annie?"

"I don't want to talk about her."

"All right, well, you must continue on with your journal. . . . For yourself, of course."

Nicola Vileroy sat alone in her room. She looked at her face in an ornately designed Victorian vanity mirror that sat atop her bedroom dresser. It used to belong to the first Mrs. Goodman-Brown. Faith, she was called. What a disgusting name. Faith. In what is a person to have faith? God? Family? The only family Nicola had ever had was a ragtag group of Egyptians to whom she was born, so many centuries ago, and her son. Edward Hyde. What a boy he was. When he was born, for an instant Nicola had felt human love. She had pushed it away, thinking that the call of destiny is a nobler feeling — bigger, capable of so much more. But here was Edward, her own flesh. Ah, but what is flesh? She had inhabited many kinds of flesh. And Edward's, too, would die away. It was better to retain his essence, his soul. And so she did.

He remained with Nicola, and he would always do so — because Nicola had found a way to preserve him. To summon him to her.

"Call me Mom," she had asked Thomas on so many occasions.

She didn't care if he complied. He wasn't her son, after all. Her own son would always come to her. He would always call her his mother. He surpassed all the children she watched, over the many decades, because he was unafraid of his own free will.

She looked at her face in the mirror again. She had surrounded her chair and the entire vanity and dresser with a thin silk mosquito net that was affixed to the ceiling. From outside it, she was only a shadow, and Charles knew not to disturb her inside the gauzy sanctuary. The school nurse was coming back again. She had to build up her strength and never let any of her new friends and family—especially the Darling children and the Lost Boys who had unveiled her—see anything of the missing nurse in the face of the magnificent Nicola Vileroy Goodman-Brown.

Though, she considered, there is something wonderful about a life with two faces. So much to be learned and accomplished when in disguise. Much like a fly on a wall.

She reached into her pocket and took out a jar of red pills. Each of them stamped with a *W*. Thomas was napping now. She would put it back before he woke up.

"Nice job, Nikki," she said aloud. Thomas would never have accepted the pills from his stepmother. He didn't trust her as he should. And he was slow in taking them. She couldn't leave such an important task in his fickle teenage hands. Her plans, her son, her very life and survival, depended on it.

She took out two of the pills and ground them up into a fine powder, using the sharp back end of an eyebrow pencil. Then she poured the powder into an open sugar packet, replaced the cork on the bottle, and set out, first to replace the bottle in Thomas's jacket pocket, then to the kitchen.

Thomas woke up later in the day, in his own bed, to the sounds of a Goodman-Brown evening. His father playing some old classic rock music on his office computer, once in a while shouting into a phone at some business partner. Either Nicola or the maid cooking in the kitchen. It must have been the maid, because he hadn't been awake for a minute before his stepmother entered his room without knocking.

"How was school?" she asked. "Did you have a good day?"

"Did you forget to knock?" he shot back. He looked down at himself. He was wearing jeans, his favorite pair, and his wallet was on the floor beside the bed.

She answered as if she thought it was a real question. "No," she said, and sat down at his desk. "You're having trouble sleeping," she said. This was definitely not a question, so he didn't bother to answer. He wondered why he was sleeping in his clothes. Had he gone out, or was he on his way out?

"What time is it?" he asked. *What day is it?*

For a moment she looked sad, as if she were sorry about something or had been disappointed. Was she trying to look more like Belle? To remind him of her existence somewhere in the world? "I'm sorry you don't like me," said Nicola. "I've tried."

He didn't know what to say to that. His stepmother had never before admitted any kind of weakness. "We both know what you said the other night," he said, forgetting about his clothes or the time. "We both know what happened back at your old apartment last year. I saw you there . . . the other night."

"I'm sorry if you misunderstood," said Nicola, with her honey-sweet French accent making every word seem tragic and sincere. "When I said those things, I thought we were just *joking around,* as they say. I thought we were bonding."

Thomas sat up in bed. Was she kidding? No, she seemed entirely serious. Had he misheard some of what she'd said, what

60

she'd implied? He had been sort of out of it lately. And it was true that he couldn't completely sleep.

"Your friend Annie called," said Nicola, her long fingers straightening out the papers on his desk. He felt uncomfortable having her touch them—his writings, his notes, the pages of his journal. But she seemed unconcerned with their contents and was busying herself with arranging them just right.

"What did she say?" He remembered now that he had forgotten to give Annie a ride home. He had promised. Thomas had been screwing up with Annie for weeks. He didn't know why he did it. He would be sweet to her, invite her and Roger out, and then suddenly do something mean and careless. Surely she was tired of it. She would never speak to him again.

"She was upset that you broke your . . . um . . . appointment," said Nicola. "I told her that you were ill and that I had told the driver to bring you home right away."

Thomas raised an eyebrow. Why would Nicola cover for him with Annie?

"She seemed to believe me," said Nicola with a conspiratorial smile. "Lucky boy. You get one more chance with the young lady."

Thomas shrugged. He rolled over on his side and closed his eyes. He could hear Nicola getting up, moving around the room. He felt invaded by her presence here, wished she would just go away. Suddenly, he felt her cold hand on his forehead. His stomach lurched. He felt a shiver run through him and he desperately wanted to pull away, but he didn't have the strength. She was leaning over him now, whispering. His whole body stiffened and he didn't dare open his eyes. He imagined what she would look like up close, if he looked up right now and peered into her face. A nightmarish vision of Belle's face suddenly overtook him. Belle's face up close, just as he was about to kiss her at the dance, turning into something monstrous and ghoulish. His body shot up, almost on its own, and he hurled Nicola's arm off him. He sat in bed, panting, his stepmother standing a foot or two away, not shocked or horrified but breaking into a curious smile.

"I've left you something on your desk," she said, "to help you sleep."

He didn't respond. He noticed the smoothie, his favorite kind, just like the one he had spilled the last time she had offered it to him.

"I asked the young lady in the kitchen to teach me how you like it," she said. "I spent a long time getting the fruits just right. And I added some lavender . . . from Provence." She smiled big, as if she was proud of this accomplishment, and suddenly Thomas felt foolish, paranoid, cruel. At the same time, she was a mystery to him — each time they talked, her behavior was completely different. He thanked her. She swept out of the room. "Good night, dear," her disembodied voice called from outside his door.

He let a few sleepless minutes pass before he pulled himself out of bed, his body aching, and looked on his desk for the smoothie. He could see chunks of unblended strawberry, exactly the way he liked it, floating all through the glass. Sometimes his new stepmother pulled the most surprising moves. Another person might even say she was cool for a mom type. The school therapist kept saying that he was imagining the random scenes from that night at the Faust home — that it was impossible, flashes of false memory resulting from his trauma over losing Belle, whom she admitted Thomas had genuinely loved. The therapist claimed that there were official records of the Faust children in their new Swiss school and that Nicola Vileroy was not capable of ridiculous things like torture or black magic. She said that Thomas's dream about Belle's face melting was a classic one after a breakup. Thomas had to admit that it all sounded ridiculous, even to his own ears.

He told himself to relax.

Then he thought of the W and began to panic. He rushed to his desk and checked his jacket pocket for the bottle. It was still there, cool and reassuring against his palm. He would have to find a good hiding place for it. He breathed out and reached for the glass. He needed nourishment now. He lifted the glass to his lips and gulped down the smoothie like a first drink of water after a marathon.

⇒≫

"It can't be true," said a female voice to his left. Thomas was walking through the halls at Marlowe, his head pounding despite a full night's sleep, trying to figure out why everyone seemed so frantic. Marlowe's halls were usually full of gossip and frenzy, but today it seemed somehow magnified. Everywhere he turned, there were whispers, fumes of everyone's energy filling the air like some noxious gas. He saw Connor in a huddle of jocks, shaking his head and saying, "Why did he go by himself in the first place?"

The jocks were wearing sports jerseys, as they always did on game days. Was today a game day? He waved at Connor, who nodded back.

A group of girls with band instruments gathered around a single iPhone, posting something on Facebook. "I bet it's just a rumor," said one of them.

"I saw Thomas jump down his throat the other day," said another one.

"I saw them take him away myself!" said a shrill-voiced girl with jet-black hair and pins all over her shirt, a goth named Marla. "You calling me a liar?" She was wearing her black street clothes instead of the Marlowe uniform. Casual clothes were allowed only on certain Fridays. . . . Not today.

Thomas squinted at Marla. She seemed energized by this firsthand news she was able to bestow upon her eager friends. He headed toward his locker, groggy eyes fixed toward the end of the hallway so he wouldn't stumble. *This has got to stop,* he told himself, though he wasn't sure what exactly he had done. He had only gone home and slept. He spotted a poster for the lacrosse game. MARLOWE VERSUS BARD TONIGHT! But the game was supposed to be on . . . Friday night. *What's wrong with me?* he thought. How many days had passed?

Somebody whispered something about the missing school nurse, about all the strange things that had happened lately.

He spotted Annie standing by herself. "What's going on?" he asked, and for once she didn't look him up and down as if he were her patient.

"It's Roger." Her voice broke as she said his name. "Everyone's talking about him, and they didn't even know he existed before today!"

"What happened?" said Thomas. What's the worst that could possibly happen to a kid like Roger?

"He went out last night," said Annie, her eyes filling with tears. "To Elixir."

"Did they catch him with a fake ID or something?" said Thomas. "It's just a slap on the wrist for that."

Annie gave him a furious look. "He went out by himself, and he was beaten up in an alley outside the club. It was really bad. No one saw the guy, but he was much bigger. Now Roger's in a coma."

Thomas tried to swallow. His mouth was dry and he wiped his lips with the back of his hand. "What day is it?" he muttered.

"What?" Annie seemed confused and insulted, like she thought he was blowing off the whole Roger issue. "What's wrong with you?"

"I'm sorry," said Thomas. "I've been really sick."

"It's Friday," she said carefully. "You missed a couple of days of school." She reached over and touched his hand. "Are you OK?" He nodded, and after a moment, she dropped his hand and started looking around again. "I don't know what's gonna happen to Roger," she whispered. "Thomas, he could die."

He put an arm around Annie's shoulder and began to lead her away. He didn't want to think about Roger or what might have happened at Elixir. Maybe it was his fault for not inviting him along. There was no way a kid like Roger could handle himself alone there. "Come on," he said to Annie. "Let's go get some breakfast."

Later that afternoon Thomas dropped his backpack, cell phone, and keys onto the kitchen table and went straight for the fridge. He felt like he hadn't eaten in days. The day had been a blur of frenzied whispers about Roger and his fight and the coma. In the back of his father's car, he had consoled Annie and promised not to disappear again — at least not so soon. After dropping her off at her apartment,

Thomas had scoured the Facebook pages of all of Roger's friends. He found no useful information about who had gone out with him last night or what exactly happened.

His head still hurt. He reached for a slice of old quiche and started on it with his fingers, not bothering to pull back the plastic wrap all the way off the plate. Everything felt strange. Even the house had an eerie darkness to it just now, a feeling of asphyxiation. He wondered if the cleaning lady had come by today.

Earlier Annie had told him that it was Friday, that he had missed a few days of school, but he didn't remember anything about the last few days. He knew he hadn't taken any W, and he certainly didn't have any other drugs lying around. He hadn't had a drink since that night at Elixir with Nikki and Connor. So why couldn't he remember?

His stepmother's voice jolted him out of his thoughts. "Don't worry," she said as she glided into the kitchen and started rearranging a vase of flowers. She shot him a careful, reassuring glance. "About last night, I mean. I covered for you with your father. See? We are friends." She moved the vase to a spot near a window, arranging each flower to catch the light. "These are from the PTA," she said with the casual air she seemed to think was motherly. "I arranged for a *notoriously* unavailable location for some fundraiser. I got lucky, really. Some wedding was canceled." Then she added as she played with her enormous pearl studs, "Poor young couple."

Thomas stopped chewing, his mouth numb, his fingers tingling. "What are you talking about?" he said, suddenly aware of his aching muscles, his stiff arms, his tired legs, the small tear on the side of his jeans — the same pair he vaguely remembered putting on in some recent memory. Had he gone out in those jeans?

Madame Vileroy raised a shapely eyebrow. "I suppose they realized they were wrong for each other, darling," she said.

Thomas glared at her. "No, I mean last night. I was sleeping in my room the entire night."

Nicola laughed. "That almost sounds convincing, dear," she said. "But you don't have to play games with me. I have a teenage son, too, you know." Then she sighed deeply and added, while plucking a dead petal from one of the roses, "No, darling. You went out last night. Don't you remember?"

6

HOUSE ARREST

The girl was born in an unremarkable town in Egypt and from the start showed signs of an unhappy, jealous, vengeful, and cunning constitution. Born in a time of gods and monsters, spells and poisons, she quickly learned to channel what we in the modern era would call demons, to find the way to communicate with those who lived in the underworld.

Mystical accounts of this region are diverse, but many believed that an earthbound demon began life as a human, usually one with a curse. Interestingly, recent finds in the Alexandrian cache of scrolls tell a piecemeal story, wherein the young girl's curse was that she was plain and unremarkable. Though she was born to a family that was already destined for legend, the young girl, Neferat, was a nothing.

She began to experiment with dark magic. She lost herself in it, the incantations and potions and black-hearted oaths. She twisted ancient curses. She dug deeper into the abyss, played with deep, untouchable dusts. She mixed fire and blood in the night.

In a portion of the Alexandrian cache, a piece of papyrus states, "She began to nurture a talent for brewing vile potions" (Shankman, p. 34).

As the myths go, her transition to a demon of the Legion was remarkably quick. As early as a few decades later, the figure is referred to as "dark one." She was in a position of great power as the pharaoh's nursemaid, able to manipulate royals and steal the Egyptian throne for her favorite. In the process, she created the fifth great injustice of her family and completed the prophecy of bonedust—a living dust made from the bones of five members of her family, mummies who died of the cruelest injustices and were ritually preserved (cf. Book of Gates, *p. 213, Simon's translation). With this fifth one, she opened a path to immortality, which she was obliged to guard when she became the Dark Lady of the underworld.*

Indeed, this bonedust—which she hid deep in the labyrinthine worlds below—was her own immortal hoard, tied closely to her ability to linger through the millennia.

Over the centuries, the demoness figure of "Neferat" steps in and out of the spotlight. In a few instances in eastern European lore, she is described as "the one-eyed witch." The phrase links Neferat to the name she adopted later—Nicola Vileroy (Russo-Hungarian Folklore, p. 12).

As Vileroy, the demon developed a capability for gathering and corrupting the souls of ambitious youths like herself. By any understanding of the "demon," this was her mission. But as men began to hunt for the immortal dust, Nicola found ways to hide pieces of the five mummies in the form of secret potions. Unlike any mythic figure before her, Vileroy created an unholy trinity — a three-fold path to her own immortality. This was Nicola's survival.

— Excerpt from chapter 2, "Origins of the Demon First Known as Neferat, Then as Nicola Vileroy," Demon Histories, *by Professor Jamie West*

Thomas spent most of that evening in his room, trying to work out what had happened to him. He had zero recollection of going out. Usually, if he'd drunk too much or had a strange pill, he could still remember the hazy outlines of the night or maybe one or two flashes of some girl he'd met or a song he'd heard. Sometimes he would remember something he had said, as if it were part of a dream. But a complete blackout? That had never happened to him . . . had it? Even Nikki's tiny miracle pills hadn't knocked him out completely. Besides, he didn't take any W last night. Maybe Nicola was lying to get him into trouble. Wasn't *that* the most likely thing? She must be messing with his mind. Probably he didn't go out at all, as Nicola said he did, and she was just trying to scare him by implying that she would tell his father. Maybe this was her way of blackmailing Thomas so he would fall in line.

After all, when you black out, you at least remember the moments before — like when you got in the car to go to a club or when you ordered the bottle or took the drug. . . .

Wait . . . Thomas now remembered the smoothie Nicola had left on his desk to help him sleep. That was the last substance he had consumed. Could she have laced it with something? It was definitely Nicola. Suddenly he felt stupid for having put something that *she* gave him into his body — Thomas knew by now that for all her games of nice-nice, she couldn't be trusted. He suspected that she was the one who had gotten him arrested on the night of the wedding in the first place. He wished he had saved some of that smoothie so that he could analyze it or something — just how would one go about dissecting a smoothie? Should he take the glass to a lab at NYU or to a scientist or someone like that? Definitely not the police — that would be inviting an investigation and a whole lot of poking around into his private business.

Whatever was going on inside his house, Thomas now swore to himself — and silently to his oblivious, duped father — that he would figure it out. Wasn't it his dream to be a lawyer one day? This was his chance to do some investigating into something that was more important than any case he would have in his future career. Better yet, this was his chance to prove to his dad that he wasn't worthless, that he hadn't gone off the rails after his mother died or when Belle left. This was his chance to show Mr. Goodman-Brown that Thomas didn't belong in the family business and that being a badly paid government-employed lawyer is a good-enough calling for the son of a tycoon.

He sat on his bed and flipped through the pages of his journal. Maybe he would write an entry about this. He felt stupid at the thought, closed the book, and hid it under a pile of debate folders in his desk. Then he remembered something. He had hidden the bottle of red pills under his mattress. Maybe he could start by checking the pills to see if he had taken any last night. He rushed to his bed and lifted the mattress. The bottle was where he had left it. It looked untouched. It hadn't even rolled from the spot he had chosen for it, exactly two inches below the mattress tag.

He poured the pellets into his hand, like Halloween candy. He had never really bothered to count them, but the bottle still looked relatively full. He dropped the pills one by one into the narrow mouth of the bottle and returned it to his pocket.

OK, so he probably hadn't taken any W. And clearly neither Nicola nor his dad had found his stash. More than likely, there was nothing wrong with the smoothie, either. That was a wild idea to start.

What else could he do?

He sat down at his desk, considered going for the journal again. But then his glance fell on the pile of debate papers and on the medals he had won over the years. And the answer floated into his mind as easily as a line in a favorite song. It was so obvious. Why hadn't he thought about it before?

Yes, he had had a blackout once before.

Yes, it was related to his new stepmother.

Last year, on the night he had dinner at the Faust home. Even though every moment of that night was accounted for in his memory, he was absolutely certain that he *did* in fact lose consciousness at some point that night. He had no proof, but he could feel it — it was the details that bugged him, the eerie perfection, the clipped conversations, the plastic look of the meal. Mostly, it was the way his memories of that night flipped from scene to scene, like a TV show. He didn't remember going to the bathroom or making a faux pas or encountering an awkward pause the entire night.

This was the answer he was looking for. To find out more about his stepmother, and maybe even discover why so much of his recent memory was missing, a good investigator would start at the beginning.

He had to visit the governess Vileroy's first home in New York.

He didn't take the car or a taxi, and he didn't bother telling his father or stepmother that he was going out. He wanted to be unseen, discreet. He couldn't risk being found out. He waited in the street outside the apartment, a place he had lingered many times last year when he was dating Belle. A row of brownstones stood shoulder to shoulder, each of them with a slightly different door, mismatched shrubs growing outside, and in a whole range of bricks. Some had just four or five big steps in the front, while others had a dozen shallow ones. Still, they matched like siblings in a row. He remembered waiting in this exact spot on that last night — the night of the big dance — when she had run away, her face a hideous mess, and he had tried to convince her to come down and talk to him. It was around midnight now, and the street was dark, an unusual thing in New York. The windows of the old Faust place looked dilapidated and unclean. He could hear insects and rodents crawling around in the gutters above, and something smelled like mildew and old garbage.

Thomas squinted to get a better look. Was there a faint light in the apartment? A quick movement just behind a thin curtain?

And why would there be curtains in an empty apartment in the first place? He knew that Vileroy still owned this place and that it hadn't been put up for sale. For some reason, no one ever asked about it, even in the tight New York real-estate market.

He ran to the other side of the street so he could peer farther in. It was hopeless. From the other side, the apartment was black, and even the thin sheet of fabric half covering the windows was invisible.

But then he saw it again, a quick flutter of light — like a kid with a flashlight zipping across a room. He jumped up to catch a glimpse. All he saw was a handful of insects flying out of the window and disappearing toward Lexington Avenue.

"I'm losing it," he whispered to no one. "I should go home."

But Thomas had come this far. He couldn't possibly leave without at least peeking into the lobby. After all, this was an expensive building with lots of rental apartments. The least he could do was talk to some neighbors or ask the doorman for a forwarding address.

Stepping into the lobby, though, the atmosphere that greeted him was not at all what Thomas had expected.

The floor was deserted. Not just deserted but a wasteland. It was musty and full of debris. The lights had burned out, except for one exposed lamp hanging from a wire in a corner. The doorman's desk was broken, even shredded in the corners, and the floor was covered in soot. There were dead bugs on the floor. It was as if the owners had given up on the building entirely, and the city had condemned it to rot . . . as if this one edifice had been forgotten, wiped off the rosters of real-estate brokers and construction companies, off the radars of all those New York builders that usually snap up city blocks and fixer-uppers like the last donut holes in a box of fat-free bran muffins.

Despite all the changes, Thomas couldn't hold back the familiar pang of dread that overcame him just by stepping into the building. This was the place where bad things had happened to him. Recently the memory of that night was repairing itself. Being back here made his head hurt the way it did that night. *What had happened?*

Nicola had been there.

Belle had tried to save him.

Victoria had done something to hurt him.

The building was abandoned. But any good lawyer would realize that people unknowingly leave loads of evidence lying around — trails of tidbits that could be used to fill in the gaps of a story — even after they desert a place forever. He decided to go upstairs and see for himself.

The elevator was probably dangerous, so he took the stairs, trying the whole time not to be afraid of what he would find once he reached the Fausts' floor. What was that flash of light he saw from the street? Was someone in the apartment right now? Maybe he had imagined it.

When he reached the front door, Thomas noticed the strangest detail so far. The door was made of a plain beige-colored wood, a completely ordinary, unsophisticated door like you would find in a public office building or an elementary school. It wasn't anything like the ornately chiseled, massive entrance that he remembered from his previous visits. Why would someone downgrade a *door*? How could this whole place have gone to hell so quickly?

He twisted the knob. Inside, a smell of rot and disease filled his nostrils so that he began coughing uncontrollably. He took a few steps inside, but he could hardly see in the thick, windowless dark. He thought he felt something fly into his open mouth.

He was about to run out of there when he heard someone speak.

"Who's there?" a frightened yet menacing voice squealed in the dark. Thomas couldn't tell if it was male or female. Maybe it was a child.

He cleared his throat. He squinted but it didn't help.

The voice spoke again. "I said, Who's there?" It was coming from across the room. He should just run, he thought. The voice continued, a little calmer than before. "Tell me why you're here, or I'll have my brother knock you out. He's right behind you."

In that fraction of a second, Thomas felt a breath on his neck. He whipped around.

A boy was standing within a foot of him, holding some kind of wooden plank. His face flickered in the candlelight for only a second — was it a face he knew? — before the plank came flying and Thomas staggered and fell to the floor. He groaned and tried to lift his head. The voices were gone now. He lay there for another ten minutes, breathing into the wooden floorboards, before he looked up and saw that he was back in the lobby.

7

CSI: MARLOWE

London, England, in the Year of Our Lord 1520

"Well, hang me if it isn't my old friend the governess. What are you doing in these dark alleys at night? It's dangerous here . . . lurking about . . ."

"I have urgent business. I need your help."

"What can an old apothecary do for a lady like you?"

"I need a baby."

"Oh, ho, ho! How very human of you. Is it not enough being governess to the upstart Boleyn family? They have daughters for you to coddle."

"It's not that. I need . . . You must swear to keep silent on pain of death."

"I will swear. But you know death means nothing to me."

"I need a baby of my own blood. A natural son to carry on my work . . . my soul."

"This is sad news, my old friend. Have you lost your link to the eternal?"

"Just tell me what I must do. This is magic too old even for me."

"Such bloody days . . . and now more blood must be spilt. Come in, come in. They've already visited me twice on account of witchcraft. I don't need more bodies here."

"Be quick. I must have a remedy or I'll lose my place in the Legion."

"I can make it so you become pregnant, and I can make it so you have a son. But do you have the stomach for what must come next?"

"Tell me. Be quick."

"The child will have your very soul. You will love him, as humans love their children. And then, on the night he turns sixteen, you must kill him. You must burn his body and mix his ashes with your previous source of immortality. This is what every demon must do when her life source begins to run out. For me, it was the waters of a spring of Eden. For you, I believe, it was the bones of five mummies of your own blood. Am I right? Yes, yes . . . I did this myself when my water began to run out. It wasn't easy, I must tell you."

"What comes next?"

"You must take the mixture containing the ashes and the life source and feed all of it to the one chosen human—the one who is worthy to carry the soul of your child forever. Then your spirit will live on in the chosen victim and in all his children, grandchildren, and the generations that follow, so that you will not only live on in him but multiply, filling the earth with a new superior race, one unencumbered by love or frailty. Then you can have your own Legion . . . unless . . ."

"Unless what?"

"Well, naturally there is an art to choosing a victim."

Thomas wondered why he was going to student council, given the monumental things going on in his own house. But what could he do? If he didn't keep up with his commitments, his dad would pull him out of school and send him to some military camp or institution for wayward boys. A calendar full of AP classes, sports, and debate matches was the only thing keeping Charles Goodman-Brown from staging a faculty-wide intervention at Marlowe on behalf of his son.

He considered what he had seen and heard at the Faust place. Somebody was still living there, in that putrid purgatory. He had heard a childish voice, and something had definitely struck him in the head. Could it have been one of the Faust kids? Or had he imagined it? He remembered a face. Should he report it to social services or to the school counselor? But if he did, what would he say? *My stepmother is some kind of witch and she has imprisoned some kids, possibly former students, in an Upper East Side lair full of dead bugs and a creepy death vibe?* Yeah, that wouldn't get him committed.

One thing was certain: Nicola Vileroy had lied about seeing Thomas go out the night Roger was attacked. She must have. Either that or she was making him forget.

Annie was standing by her locker. She had her head so deep in there that he could see only her lower half as she fumbled to pull out something from the back. He approached and tapped her on the shoulder. She jumped back.

"Sorry," said Thomas, looking at his watch. "Do you have to get to class?"

"No. Actually, I was waiting for you," said Annie. "Have you heard anything else about Roger? I was wondering if maybe you could get me into Elixir to investigate."

"Um," said Thomas, immediately defensive. "No, that's not a good idea, Annie. You shouldn't go there."

"Why not?" she said, her tiny arms crossed. "You go there all the time. Besides, I've decided to figure out for myself what happened to Roger. Everyone's being so useless . . . acting like once he gets better it doesn't matter if we ever figure out who did it."

"Is he getting better?" said Thomas, itching to change the subject.

"No," she said. "He's still in a coma. I want to figure out who did it before he wakes up, so he doesn't have to be scared."

Thomas smiled and put an arm around her shoulder. "That's really nice."

She shrugged. "He's my best friend," she said. "I have some theories. I think it probably had to do with Roger being gay, don't you? I know it's hard to imagine it nowadays, but that stuff still happens. Right?"

Thomas wondered if he had heard her right. Did she say *gay*? Roger? "Wait," he said. "But he likes you. I mean . . . I thought he was jealous and that's why he didn't like me. . . ."

The look on Annie's face was a mix of disgust, confusion, and embarrassment. "Oh, he'd have to be jealous not to like you?" She must have realized that the comment was a low blow, because then she shook her head, smiled feebly, and said, "Sorry. No, he wasn't into me like that. But you're probably right that he was jealous of all the time you and I spent together."

Thomas felt like a tool. All this time, he had wanted Roger out of the way, thinking that he was trying to move in on his girl. But all Roger wanted was to keep from losing his best friend. Why had Thomas never known this about Roger? Thomas had to admit to himself that he had basically just failed to pay attention.

But was Roger's beating really about being gay? Thomas didn't want to think about it anymore. The idea that he had wished Roger any harm was too much, given everything that had happened.

"Look, I have to go," he said to Annie.

"So will you take me to Elixir?"

"I don't know, maybe." With that, he bounded down the hall toward the student-council meeting room.

The halls of Marlowe were mostly empty by five p.m. Sports were winding down for the day, and now that the sun was disappearing earlier and earlier, no one was all that eager to drag out their after-school activities. Thomas was leaving the student-council room, trying to shove the fifty or so handouts that Lucy Spencer had printed—prom flyers and fund-raiser announcements and petitions for various causes—into his backpack, when he spotted the single light dotting the long, dim hallway. It was coming from the principal's office. He could see from across the empty corridor that at least two people were inside, talking in hushed voices that drifted in patches through the half-open door.

He crept closer. Something made him curious — maybe it was the lateness of the meeting or the furtive quality of the voices. Or maybe it was just that Thomas had a lot of secrets lately. As he approached the office, he noticed a black box propped just inside the door, holding it ajar. It was one of those police investigation tool kits.

Inside, he heard familiar voices.

One was Principal Stevenson's, but there were two others — both of them strangely out of place here in Marlowe.

"Yeah, it's a real shame, but we've got no choice. It's gotta happen by the book."

A sickening feeling overtook Thomas. It was the voice of the police commissioner named Paulie, the same one who had come to his father's wedding, made a huge scene, arrested him, and then left him to rot in the police station.

The second police officer spoke now, in a more deferential tone than the first.

"Sure, it might disrupt the flow of things before and after school, but we'll try to do most of our investigating when the kids are in class."

It was Detective Mancuso. *What luck,* Thomas thought. As if he didn't have enough people breathing down his neck at home, now his two arresting officers were going to be spending their days at Marlowe. He wondered if they would search the dorm rooms. Was that legal? He should warn Cornrow and the other boarding guys.

"Here's the thing," said Commissioner Paulie. "This case has now been upgraded to a hate crime. Do you understand what that means?"

There was no answer, which made Thomas think that Principal Stevenson was nodding or shaking his head.

"We've spoken to the victim's parents, as well as some of his friends, and we believe that the perpetrator was motivated by Roger's sexual orientation. Since Elixir is a new hot spot for the private-school crowds around here, we also believe that the perp was some-one who knew the boy. Possibly the whole thing was planned out in advance." The commissioner cleared his throat. "Of course, that means we have to take it much more seriously than your run-of-the-mill assault."

"We have a zero-tolerance policy toward hate crimes," said Detective Mancuso. "We want to devote two detectives to this full-time, to investigate Marlowe for as long as it takes to find the assailant."

"Yes, yes," said Principal Stevenson. "Do what you have to do."

"Good," said Commissioner Paulie. "We're gonna smoke out the bastard."

8

DOUBLE YOU

London, England, in the Year of Our Lord 1536

Two women walk in a manor field, near a grove of English elms —
one woman a gaunt brunette, unsteady on her feet, holding some
unfinished embroidery work, the other woman blond, rigid, and pos-
sessed of an evil eye. "Governess, I've miscarried again. Again. Henry
is mad with grief. He thinks I deceived him into marriage by sorcery."

"Well," says the governess, "didn't you? We've gotten you the
English crown, Anne. Do try to be grateful."

"He's going to kill me," says the brunette. "He has a younger mis-
tress. I used to be the younger mistress. Now I've failed three times to
bear a son. . . ."

Night is getting on as the two walk across the hunting grounds,
toward a waiting carriage. A footman opens the door of the carriage,
bows, and speaks. "Do you approve of the manor, Your Majesty?"

"Henry made a fine purchase," says the young queen as she steps
into the carriage. The footman closes the door. The queen turns to the

governess. "We would have named this park after our son. Henry the Ninth Park."

"If not your son," says the governess, "then mine."

"You have a son?"

The governess evades: "If I did, I would name him Hyde, and this land after him."

"Hyde Park? It sounds ridiculous. . . . It needs a royal name."

"You are right, my queen."

The queen puts the unfinished embroidery up to her lips, to stifle a sob. The driver mounts the carriage. The queen leans out of the window and whispers, "Governess, please. Will you help me stay young?"

The eye of the governess seems to shimmer. Her mouth, a straight line, tilts upward into a grin. "But why, Anne? Why would I ever do that?"

The carriage pulls away, down the king's private road at Hyde Manor. The governess stands by a sycamore and watches the sun fade. A lingering shadow emerges from behind the tree. The governess speaks without turning around: "Did you retrieve the bonedust?"

"Yes," says the shadow.

"Good boy," says the governess.

"But an Egyptian boy has stumbled upon it as well. He took the last one."

"So kill him."

"He was very quick."

The governess is silent. The figure in the shadow holds his breath.

"Edward," says the governess, "we have only a superficial mask for this aging. With the bonedust, we can cure it. It is the source of our immortality. If you can't get it for me, dear boy, or protect it from *some dim-witted child, then I won't have enough for the both of us, and I'll be forced to grind you into little tablets. You'll be all that I have left, Edward. Is that what you want?"*

"No, Mother."

"That's a good boy."

Thomas knew he was asleep. You can't fly to Ibiza in the time it took for him to get there. He was playing golf. He remembered that much. On a course somewhere, his coach giving him the happy voice — the one he used when Thomas was slamming drives so far that they needed NASA clearance. He was on the fairway at Pebble Beach. No, no, wait. He saw that on TV. He was practicing with the Marlowe team at the driving range on Chelsea Piers, looking out onto the Hudson River. His coach said, "You're hittin' the pigeons, Goodman-Brown. You're bombing the moon!"

Pigeons are birds. The Canary Islands are near Ibiza. Then he was in Ibiza. Ibiza is in Spain. The club in Ibiza is outdoors with netting above the dance floor. Paper lanterns hang from the nets; the ocean water is lapping somewhere against the rocks. Everybody has that sun-sleep smell. Half the girls just walked in from the beach, wearing colorful little skirts over their swimsuits. Thomas is dancing. Flashing lights. A girl smiling at him. A golf club swinging and smacking the ball into the air. A back alley in New York, someone huddled on the ground, taking kicks to the stomach. The sound of a jet. The smiling girl is Nikki.

Where are you going, Nikki? He should have gotten her last name.

Pretty, smiley Nikki . . . Sounds sort of like Nicola . . . Same bluish eyes, too . . . except Nicola's smiles are fake and scary and make him want to run away.

The scenes flickered across his vision too fast. Thomas closed his eyes. Behind his eyelids it was the Fourth of July. What month was it? He squeezed the visions away.

When he opened his eyes, he awoke in a courtroom. The fluorescent lights were too bright. The table in front of him, the judge's bench, the jurors' box — they were all the same color wood. Thomas blinked. It might have taken a day. When he opened his eyes again, he was still in the court. Everyone was looking at him. The jury was a commercial for racial diversity. Thomas knew there was sound, because he heard a woman clear her throat behind him. Finally, the judge said, "Is that all, Mr. Goodman-Brown?"

All Thomas could think was, *Holy crap, I hope I have my pants on.* He looked down. Good news. Pants were on.

"Mr. Goodman-Brown?" said the judge.

Thomas looked up. "I'm sorry, what?"

The courtroom stirred. For the first time, Thomas read the crest hanging from the judge's bench. It said, THE UNITED STATES SUPREME COURT.

But the Supreme Court doesn't have a jury, thought Thomas. He looked to his left. There was no jury. Not even a jurors' box. He looked up front again; this time, nine judges sat in front. It was the Supreme Court. Thomas was doubly glad that his pants were on.

"I said, Will that be all, Counselor?" said the judge. "Does the defense rest?"

"Oh!" said Thomas. It seemed he was the defense lawyer. *Score!* "Yes, Your Honor. The defense rests."

The other eight judges sighed and sat back from the edge of their seats. The center judge said, "Well, Mr. Goodman-Brown, if someone had told me yesterday that a young man such as yourself was going to defend the single most important piece of judicial review this country has ever seen, I would have been dubious. But that, young man, was one effing genius closing statement. This court has no choice but to rule in favor of such pimpical lawyering."

The courtroom erupted with cheers. Two of the female judges gave each other high fives. The old judge in the corner began the slow clap.

Thomas raised both fists into the air as a little newspaper boy from the 1920s ran into the courtroom, shouting, "Extra! Extra! Top lawyer Thomas Goodman-Brown voted Most Likable Man in America!"

Thomas woke up. He was on the floor of his room with his shirt off. A golf ball was in his pocket, digging into his leg. At first he thought he'd slept on a golf club, but then realized it was his left arm. It was so numb, he couldn't tell it was his. He tried to groan, but his tongue was stuck to the side of his mouth. He rolled over. The room was dark, except for his desk lamp. His alarm clock said it was nine thirty, but it could have been morning or evening. He had no idea. He didn't even know what day it was.

"Your father and I missed you at dinner." Madame Vileroy's voice startled Thomas, but his reflexes were so addled that he didn't move. She was sitting on his bed, in the dark.

He said, "Unnhhn hrrrr?"

His stepmother responded, "I didn't want the light to burn your eyes. Seems you've been enjoying yourself the last few days."

Thomas scraped the grime off his tongue with his teeth and swallowed as much of it as he could. He said, "Days?"

"You've been in and out," said Madame Vileroy. "If your father hadn't had an emergency at the office, he would have handcuffed you to his wrist."

Thomas pulled himself up and sat with his back against the wall, facing his bed. He dragged a palm over his face. That was when he noticed the plastic bracelets dangling from his wrist. "How did I get these?"

"The doormen at the clubs, I presume," said Vileroy.

A few of them were in Spanish; one was in Thai. Straining his eyes to read the bracelets was enough to send shooting pains through his temple. Why was Nicola in his room, anyway? Where the hell was his dad? An office emergency? He didn't even have time to punish the crap out of his son for clubbing nonstop for God knows how many days? Not that Thomas *wanted* to be punished, but at least that would be normal.

The last few days, Thomas had been starting to have black spells — little moments here and there when he would feel like he wasn't the only one in his own head. As if his body was a container and he wasn't the only thing filling it anymore.

Thomas tried to get up, but his feet were still noodles. Nicola stood up and walked over to him. She was wearing a dress that Thomas could have sworn was originally his mom's. Was it possible that his dad had allowed her to raid the closet? Maybe it was a different dress. She even smelled like Thomas's mother. She helped

Thomas stand and move to the bed. She held him by the elbow and said in a raspy whisper, "Victoria and Valentin have been asking about you."

Thomas wrenched his arm away. *"What?"* Another wave of pain shot through his temples, so that he almost fell backward. His stepmother caught him. "I only said that your friends, Connor and Annie, have been asking about you."

Thomas peered into her eye, but the pain was too strong, and in the end, he didn't care if she knew that he'd visited her house. But did she just say *Victoria and Valentin*? Were they the ones he had run into? He wished he could remember the face of the kid who had knocked him out. He would figure it out, he promised himself. Unlike the Faust kids, Thomas couldn't be disposed of without any-one knowing—absentee or not, his father would know. As he col-lapsed on top of the bedspread, he felt the golf ball in his pocket and heard it rattle. He pulled it out. It wasn't a golf ball, but the bottle of W, almost half empty.

Suddenly, he had the overwhelming desire to take one and return to his dreams.

Madame Vileroy pulled the comforter over Thomas. She said, "There's a glass of water on the nightstand. You should really take something for that headache."

As she left, Thomas popped the cap on the bottle and reached for the water. . . .

⟿

Thomas was back in the Elixir Club. It had an island theme. Maybe the owner had been to Ibiza recently. Did they go together? Thomas swaggered up to the doorman, a Russian mixed martial artist, gave him a fist pound, slid a hundred-dollar bill in the man's breast pocket, and said, "Just the tens tonight, Ivan. Nothing but tens. . . . Maybe a nine-point-five if she's smiling."

Ivan gave the best nod he could, considering he didn't have a neck, and said, "Yes, Mr. Brown."

The name — Mr. Brown — sounded weird to Thomas's ear. He shrugged and continued toward the bar. A couple of party promoters were greasing up the Wall Street crowd with complimentary bottles of the cheap stuff. A table of post-op heiresses were sipping laxative cocktails and glaring at the Brazilian models on the dance floor with enough envy to crash a Facebook account. The rich cougars were overdressed. The even richer cocaine dealers were underdressed. Some Malaysian kid texting in the corner booth was supposedly the hottest artist in Chelsea.

The headache was long gone. Vileroy and the wedding weren't even a memory. Thomas approached the glowing red bar and looked at his reflection in the mirror along the back wall. Something was different. He didn't have a chance to look closer. The cute bartender saw him and dropped a shot in the lap of two dot-com millionaires (who were desperately hitting on her) in the rush to get to Thomas.

"Hey, Tara," he said. "Do I look different to you?"

Tara was in her twenties, just out of Tisch Theatre, with a starlet's face and a stuntwoman's body. The black corsets the club used for uniforms would have been sleazy if there was even the slightest impression that Tara was available. She wasn't.

"You look tasty," she said. "Your breath smells a little."

"Really?" said Thomas, raising an eyebrow. He knew this line already.

"Yeah," said Tara, leaning over the bar. She grabbed the collar of the Prada suit and kissed him. Her mouth tasted like spearmint. As she pulled away, she said, "I'll mix your favorite. The good stuff in the back."

Tara disappeared into a back room. The dot-com guys down the bar stood with mouths hanging open.

Thomas blew out a breath. It was so cold he could see it in the air.

Wait. The last part might have been a chewing gum commercial.

Thomas shook his head. He looked in the mirror again. He did look different. His eyes were darker. They didn't even look blue anymore. That could have been the club lighting, though. His forehead seemed to extend farther out, over his eyes. His eyebrows were thicker and lower. Thomas shrugged it off. A change didn't seem like such a bad thing at this point.

The Brazilian models left the dance floor and sashayed up to the bar. The entire club watched, as if it was the Victoria's Secret runway show. By the time they reached the bar, half a dozen guys were buying them drinks. One of them saw Thomas, and he pretended not to notice as she sidled up next to him. She had on a little black dress, black ballet slippers with ribbon crisscrossing up her calves, and nothing else. No purse. No jewelry. Just perfect skin. As if she had spirited up from the ground, out of nowhere. When she glanced back a second time, Thomas was looking at her. She smiled.

"What's your name?" said Thomas.

"Carmina."

"Nice to meet you, Carmina. My name is Edward."

⟶⟵

Thomas woke from the lancing pain in his forehead and bit down on the inside of his cheek. He started to taste blood in his mouth. His tongue felt like beef jerky. His eyes flapped opened. The corneas had a dry film that scraped his eyelids.

The mornings-after just kept getting worse.

The ceiling was different. It had some cursive script painted on it that said *To Thine Own Self Be True*—this wasn't his room. The fog of sleep evaporated. Something was weighing him down. He lifted his head until his chin touched his bare chest. It was a girl. All he could see was the top of her head, but she was nestled up next to him. Her arm was draped over his chest. His left arm was under her—and totally numb.

He looked around the room. It was dark. Not just because of the night but because it had been painted dark colors, blacks and purples. On a nearby desk, a tiny white cotton doll, human shaped but completely featureless, glowed from the inside. It looked like a tiny spirit. On its head, which was about the size of an egg, two black dots of different shapes and sizes marked the eyes.

Thomas noticed more dolls around the room. On the footboard of the bed. On the floor by the door.

Blank little spirits with inky eyes.

One of them sat on a bookshelf covered with other knickknacks that Thomas could barely make out. A plaster skull glinted back the dull light in its gemstone eyes. The porcelain scales on the underside of a dragon statuette shimmered like fire in its belly. A geode opened its crystalline maw and devoured the rest of the light. Behind it were other figures, lost in the darkness.

The spirits seemed to pulsate. Were they from a movie he'd seen? Thomas felt panic rising in his chest. The nightmarish room was beginning to close in on him. *Vileroy,* thought Thomas. She must have brought him here—some kind of evil dungeon. He lifted himself on his right elbow and craned his neck to see the rest of the room.

Then he saw the image on the sidewall. It was a person—a close-up face of a boy with gelled black hair, eyeliner, and purple lipstick. He was looking up at Thomas with a disaffected glare. Above his head was a Gothic-typeface banner:

Samson Diablo: The Emo King of Spain

In concert ONE NIGHT ONLY @ Madison Square Garden

*** Dress as your favorite goth character or pagan idol to be eligible
for a door prize, courtesy of Diablo™ himself!**

Wait . . . Maybe he still had W in his system. No, it couldn't be the W. Everything felt so easy when he took it; he felt relaxed, and charming—every pill a different emotion, like pieces of a person, someone more confident than himself, as if the bottle contained the full range of that one person's concrete personality. But this was just surreal. The sleeping girl began to stir. Thomas tried to pull his left arm out from under her while she adjusted her position, but it was too numb to move on its own. He had no choice but to wake her. He reached over to the nightstand and turned on the lamp.

The light shone on the girl's face.

Thomas said, "Aw, crap."

It was Marla. The resident angry goth girl of the Marlowe School. Thomas yanked the comforter away. She wasn't naked. Neither was Thomas. Thank Diablo™.

Thomas's chest was covered in purple lipstick, but his pants were still on. She was in her underwear.

As Marla stirred and shifted, Thomas pulled his arm away and began to rub the blood back into it. He rolled out of the bed to hunt for his shirt.

Marla took a deep breath and said, "It's not morning yet."

"Uh, yeah, hi, Marla."

Thomas just wanted to get his shirt and get out of there. For all he knew, Marla had already texted pictures to half the school. He thought of Annie — the regret was worse than his headache. Why was he always hurting her? Maybe it was true what the therapist said — that he was sabotaging all his relationships since Belle.

Whatever it was, he could analyze it when he got home. For now, he needed the shirt. He lifted a pillow. Under it was his left shoe.

Marla sat up. "You threw the other one by the door," she said.

"Thanks," said Thomas. This was deeply uncomfortable. "So, Marla," said Thomas, "did we . . . ?"

Marla smirked. "Come on, Goody Brown, say it."

"You know what I mean," said Thomas.

"No, I don't."

"Did we . . . you know?"

"Bump uglies?"

"Yeah."

"No," said Marla. "Even smashed out of your mind on W, you kept it PG-13."

Thomas let out a breath. He walked over to the door and picked up the other shoe. "That's good," he said. "I just don't want it to be weird between us. We don't really know each other, and we go to the same school, and, well, I've got . . ."

"You've got little girlfriend Annie to worry about? Your squeaky reputation?"

Thomas already felt like a grade-A dickhead. Now he was insulting Marla, too.

"Look, I'm really sorry."

"Don't be sorry to me, Golden Boy," sneered Marla. "It was a hard PG-13. You done right by me, as far as I'm concerned."

Thomas didn't want to know what she meant by that. He flicked the light switch. Marla's room looked like a Renaissance festival. His shirt was still nowhere to be found. A thought interrupted Thomas's search.

"Wait a second," he said. "How did you know about W?"

Marla rolled her eyes. She leaned over the side of the bed and grabbed the crumpled-up shirt. "I know way more than that," she said. She threw the shirt at Thomas. "I know little Mister Goodman-Brown took a walk in the woods, found himself itching for a hate crime, and beat Roger into a coma. And I know he's addicted to a designer drug nobody's heard of. And I know you giggle when goth girls nibble on your earlobes."

Thomas didn't move. Had he told her the night before? When did they meet up? All he could remember was the Brazilian model named Carmina. How much had he forgotten?

96

"That's a lie," stammered Thomas. "I never hit Roger. That was just . . ."

"Sure, whatever," said Marla. "You don't need to kiss me good-bye or anything."

For the first time, Thomas looked Marla in the eyes. Her tough shell wasn't so convincing as she sat half naked in her bed. Thomas imagined that she must like him — even a little — for this to have happened. And now he was acting like she had Ebola. Thomas turned to leave. "I'm really sorry," he said over his shoulder.

"I told you not to be sorry. I'm not gonna tell anyone, if that's what you're thinking. You don't have to kiss my ass," said Marla, but she didn't sound so tough.

Thomas walked into the hall and snuck out of the Upper East Side apartment. It was only a couple blocks from his house. He crossed the street on a red light — a cab screeched its brakes to avoid hitting him. The cabbie honked his horn. Thomas didn't notice. Inside his head, he could hear someone else's voice.

It said, *She knows about us, Thomas.*

And Thomas found himself actually answering, "Yes, she does, Edward."

TWO-FACE

"*Thomas? Thomas? Do you hear me? Don't you dare leave me alone in here, Thomas. You don't want me to get angry, do you?*"

"Go away! I don't know who you are."

"*Of course you do. I'm you . . . only better.*"

"Oh, God, I'm losing it. I'm losing my mind."

"*Stop being dramatic. Everyone talks to his better self at night, when no one is there to hear it. Just listen to me now. I have something cool to show you.*"

"No! Go away. I don't want to see any more of it."

"*Sure you do. Something to be proud of. Let's look at the pictures again . . . all our best memories. Remember Roger? How he cried? . . .*"

"NO!"

"*Remember the fourth time we kicked him in the gut? He puked himself.*"

"It wasn't me. It wasn't me. Oh, God, let me sleep."

"*Sleep's for wimps. Let's go out and have some fun.*"

"No, please, Edward. Leave me alone. I can't look at it anymore. I can't live with this."

"Don't worry, you wuss. You won't remember this when we wake up. You're not ready for us to be properly introduced. Not just yet."

Holy crap. Who is Edward? Why do I keep thinking of that name?

Thomas wasn't typically prone to freak-outs, but this was insanity. He was changing. He knew it. How else do you explain hooking up with the local goth girl without any memory of it whatsoever? How else do you explain what he saw in the mirror at the bar? The name Edward, which he said aloud as he walked home from Marla's? Nothing made sense.

What he needed was to lose himself in Manhattan—no parents, no teachers, no drivers. He hadn't done that in months, and today was one of those crisp late-fall Sundays that are warm enough for just a light jacket. He had so much to think about, and he had to admit that this was the first day in a long time that he was sober enough to consider the freakiness of it all. He started near the waterside office buildings and sandwich shops in the Financial District. This was where his father wanted him to end up—crunching numbers and merging companies. But his future career was hardly a worry now that . . . Could he bring himself to think it? His stepmother . . . what was she? What had she done to him last year? And why did her apartment building look like the set from a horror movie? Could she be a witch? Or some other kind of supernatural thing? It was ludicrous. He decided soon after returning from the Faust apartment that he had hallucinated most of it—the dilapidated building, the eerie feeling, the door, the dead bugs, the knock to the head.

Maybe Nicola Vileroy was dabbling in some kind of voodoo or playing manipulative games, but she wasn't supernatural. She couldn't be.

He strolled up through Chinatown and Little Italy, stopping only for a chicken dumpling and a cannoli. After an hour of meandering, he found himself in a new cake shop in the East Village that his mom would have liked. He felt too sick for cake. His mind kept drifting back to Marla. She knew about the W. She thought *he* was the one who had attacked Roger. What if she wanted some kind of revenge for the failed hookup and tried to pin it on him? What if she told the cops? And what if they believed her? The name Edward kept flashing in his mind. He would ask himself questions and then he would answer them, as if he were talking to someone. Was that evidence of psychosis?

He decided to cut a sharp left and head west, all the way to Chelsea Market for a taco at his favorite T-shirt-store-turned-bistro. He ate alone at a table near a pant rack. He didn't feel weird about it. Thomas ate alone all the time. He wedged some more avocado slices into his taco. Strange. He had never craved avocado before. As he brought the taco to his mouth, he noticed that it seemed much smaller than before. *Stingy jerks,* he thought, always skimping on portions and raising prices. But wait . . . Was the taco really smaller? He put it down and looked at his hands, moved them up and down across the table, as though measuring the length of it. No, it wasn't that his food had shrunk. It was that his hands were bigger. Why were his hands swollen? They were a shade pastier, too.

100

What's the matter, Thomas?

Shut up! Shut up! It was as if every few seconds, someone else would occupy his brain and then leave again.

Edward. Edward. Who was he? He had heard the name before it started popping up in his head. Did he know someone named Edward from school?

He hopped into a cab after lunch. Midtown was a wasteland — walls of yellow cabs blowing exhaust into hot-dog stands, miles of cell-phone shops and cheap black suits. As the cab sped uptown, he glanced at himself in the dirty window. Was that his face? Had his jaw always been so prominent? His brow so low over his eyes? His fingers trembled as he brought them up to his face, but he didn't dare touch. He felt stronger now, a surge of bravado and excitement overtaking him as he tried to remember what he took last night. His breath grew quicker and he felt a slow hatred brewing in his chest. He could see himself punching something in the dark. Fists, blood, screaming. Someone begging for his life.

Please, Thomas. Please, stop!

Thomas looked away, suddenly frightened. He was panting hard, so the driver furrowed his brow and stared at him through the rearview mirror. Thomas asked the cabbie to drop him off at Sixtieth and Fifth, so he could walk up through Central Park and then back home. When he reached into his pocket to pay, his hands rolled across the bottle of W. The pills clinked in the jar.

Come to think of it, all of these problems had started when W came into his life. He wished he could find Nikki and ask her a few things. What was W made of? Why did it make him crazy? And why couldn't he stop taking it? It didn't shock him that he'd hooked up with Marla and forgotten about it. But was it possible for a drug to cause someone's hands to grow or their skin to fade?

No, that's stupid. . . . There's no such thing as a drug changing a person's body.

Wait a minute.

Thomas stopped dead. A woman walking behind him ran her baby stroller right into Thomas's legs. He mumbled an apology but didn't look at her.

He *did* know of someone whose face had changed. Belle! His ex-girlfriend had changed her face entirely. He had seen it for himself the night of the spring dance when she turned into a monster before his eyes. His face was changing just as Belle's had. And who did the two of them have in common? Nicola Vileroy. He had blacked out twice in his life, and both times he could link the event directly to her. Thomas had to know what W was. He clutched the bottle in his hand and started to jog back toward Marlowe. It was Sunday, but he knew one person who would be at school — just the person he needed.

***

Thomas could hear John Darling banging around in the basement all the way from the main entrance. Ever since the weird insect infestations and unexplainable leaks that had happened at Marlowe in the early fall, the basement had been boarded up. Recently, though, Professor Darling, John's father, had converted it into a science lab, where his son spent his time doing experiments and Twittering about them on his phone.

Thomas dashed down the steps leading into the basement, but

John didn't notice. He was digging in a huge cardboard box of old test tubes and beakers, cursing as he pulled out the broken ones and tossed them into a pile.

"John!" Thomas called out. "Hey, kid!"

John looked up, his face flushed. When he saw Thomas, he seemed confused at first, then scared, as if he expected that Thomas had come here on a Sunday just to stick his head in a toilet. "You're not supposed to be here," he said. "I've got a weekend pass and I've gotta go home anyway. It's almost dinner."

"Dinner?" said Thomas. "No . . . no, it's only like two p.m." Thomas remembered having just come from lunch at the T-shirt restaurant. But, come to think of it, he did feel hungry again. His clothes smelled funny, as if he had been sweating, and looking up at the tiny single window in the upper corner of the basement wall, he could see it was already dark. He touched his forehead. His head was throbbing again.

"Whatever," said John. "You can't be in here."

"Relax," said Thomas, deciding to ignore the fact that the clock seemed to have jumped ahead six hours without his knowledge. "I need help." His voice sounded wrong.

John's eyes grew round. "Um . . . OK."

Thomas tried to wipe his brow, but the feeling of his hand enveloping his face sent a jolt of fear through his body.

"You OK?" said John. "You look weird. Do you have allergies or something? Because in seventh grade, I got stung by a bee and my face got all swollen and I —"

"Shut up," Thomas interrupted. He thrust a shaking hand into his pocket and took out the bottle. He held it between two fingers, thinking he might crush it. "I need you to look at one of these under a microscope or something. I need to know what it is."

At the sight of the pills, John glanced over his shoulder to make sure no one was looking. "Where'd you get that?" he whispered. "I'm not touching that. You think you can just waltz in here with your highly sketchy jar of unmarked pills and just demand stuff? What if someone sees you? I know you're on drugs. I was at your dad's wedding." He added the last bit rather proudly. "This isn't a meth lab, rich boy."

Thomas sighed. He was about to lose all patience, but John was the only person he could trust who actually had the equipment and brains to help him. "Please," said Thomas, hating that he had to beg the nerdling for anything. "John, if you help me and don't ask questions, I'll give you whatever you want."

John looked interested. "Like . . . what?"

"Anything you can think of . . . within reason."

"Twenty wall posts," said John. "And not links or tags that make fun of me. Real friend stuff."

"Five," sighed Thomas. "I don't even do Facebook that much anymore."

"Twenty," said John, his voice high with excitement. "You said *anything*."

"Fine," said Thomas. He tapped a pill onto his palm and started to hand it to John.

"Not all in one day," said John, tapping his foot, arms still crossed.

"OK, fine," sighed Thomas.

"And you have to do the first one now. Go ahead. . . ." John held his phone out to Thomas, who, fighting the urge not to crush it in his swollen fist, logged into his own account and wrote, **Hey, John. Nice profile pic.**

Peering over his shoulder, John beamed. He took the pill and held it up to the yellow artificial light from the single bulb over the lab equipment. Then he set the pill on the wooden table that held all the microscopes and most of the beakers and made a big, long show of popping on his gloves, adjusting his goggles, and situating himself on his rolling stool. Thomas tried not to lose his temper, but it was getting difficult.

John stared at the pill under a microscope. "Huh," he said after a long time.

"What is it?" said Thomas. It was hard watching the pill in John's hands. He wanted it back in his pocket, safely in the jar with the others. He hated having it out of his control. "If you can't tell, just give it back."

John held up a hand as if he were about to find the cure for cancer and Thomas was breaking his concentration.

"Well," said John, never looking up from the microscope lens, "judging from the texture" — he sighed deeply — "the striations, and the molecular composition . . . I would say . . . that . . ." He waited another thirty seconds, adjusting the settings on the microscope a few times, before he finished. "It may as well be a breath mint. We need to break it down chemically."

That was the last straw. Thomas had now put up with this jackass for twenty minutes, and he was in no mood to play. He lunged at John, thinking only of getting back his precious tablet. John took a step back, then abruptly reached for the microscope as if to save it from Thomas.

John made his grab just as Thomas was reaching for the W. The two of them struggled over the microscope.

"Let go, you goon!" John shouted. "You'll wreck it!"

But Thomas wasn't listening. He saw John's hand over the W and he was livid. All he could think of was this weaselly kid trying to take it from him. What if he popped it in his mouth right now? What if he took the pill to Principal Stevenson and the cops?

He tried to push John's hand away from the microscope. He didn't mean to hurt him. He heard a loud grunt coming from somewhere — was it coming from his own mouth? He grabbed John's arm. As John tried to pull away, Thomas's nails dug into his flesh. John yanked hard, and as he did so, Thomas scratched his arm all the way down to the palm of his hand. John screamed.

Blood trickled over the microscope and onto the table.

Thomas stepped back, frightened at what he had done.

John was clutching the W in his palm.

"Give it back!" said Thomas.

But John wasn't paying attention anymore. "Oh . . . my . . . God," he whispered, looking down at his palm.

"What is it?" said Thomas. "What are you babbling about? Give me my pill!"

John didn't look up. He clutched his bloody arm with his other hand. The W was soaked in blood, but it rested there, unharmed. Thomas could see it now. Slowly, the blood was disappearing.

The scratch on John's hand was healing, all the way up his arm.

"What's going on?" said Thomas.

John's face had gone completely white. "I know what's in the pill!"

~~~✂~~~

Fifteen minutes later, the two boys sat on the floor in a corner of the basement, trying to calm down. Thomas had explained to John where he had gotten the pills. In return, John was telling some crazy story about something called bonedust.

"It feels so familiar," John kept saying. "It feels almost exactly the same." He kept looking at the scar on his hand, where the scratch hadn't completely healed. He touched his palm and opened and closed his fist. "It can't be a hundred-percent pure bonedust, because that healed a giant gash in my arm. And this . . . you can still see the scar. Plus, with bonedust, if you took it like you've been doing with the pills, you'd become immortal."

"Um . . ." Thomas couldn't think of anything to say.

"Remember all the weird stuff that happened at school earlier in the fall?" said John. Thomas nodded. "Well, it wasn't mold or bugs. The school was sort of . . . Promise you'll believe me?" Thomas nodded again. "The school was possessed."

Thomas laughed.

"Fine, don't believe me." John started to get up, but Thomas grabbed his arm.

"Just finish, OK?"

"My sister and I and that RA who got fired were looking for five mummies whose bones could make you immortal. It was called bonedust."

"The RA?" said Thomas. "That was the guy that stole Wendy from Connor."

"Yeah," said John. "Hey, I liked Connor way better. But anyway, the guy had been searching out bonedust for years. He found it, too, but it was all destroyed. I don't know how it's possible for some of it to have ended up in your pills. Unless—"

"Unless what?"

"Remember the missing school nurse?"

"Yeah," said Thomas. The school nurse had disappeared a month or two before, without notice, without a word. She just left, and no matter how much the school administration searched for her, no one ever found out where she was.

"She was the one trying to keep us from getting the bonedust," said John. "Maybe she had a little left. Maybe she's the one who put some of it in your pills."

Thomas rested his head against the wall. So now it was the school nurse. Where would he find her? Did she have something to do with Nikki? He was mulling everything over when John said, "I don't know why she'd give you bonedust for free, though. Like I said, that stuff is the fountain of youth."

"Fountain of youth . . ." Thomas repeated. What did it have to do with him, with his pills, with Nikki, and his stepmother? As he was considering all the possibilities, he noticed that John was back on his iPhone. Thomas was about to say something, to warn him that he should keep the W absolutely secret, when John jumped up.

"Dude, this hate crime thing is getting scary," he said as he typed something into one of his social networking sites.

"What are you talking about?" Thomas groaned. His head was

hurting again. He had woken up only a few hours ago, and here he was, ready to go back to sleep.

"People are saying that the police are coming back tomorrow," said John. His voice was part excited, part terrified. "Marla the goth chick disappeared a few hours ago. Snatched right from her bedroom!"

10

The Killing Game

Journal entry #22

My psychologist wants me to call her Dr. *Alma, even though I asked if she could perform a tracheotomy and she goes, "I'm not* that *kind of doctor, Thomas," and I said, "Well, if we're stuck on a train and some fat tourist chokes on his pretzel, and the conductor shouts, 'Help, we need a doctor!' and you can't help the dying obese guy any more than the useless fine-arts student next to you, then YOU ARE NOT A DOCTOR."*

And she purses her lips, looks at her watch, and says, "Time's up."

Meanwhile, she runs her hand through her sandy hair, rubbing her cheekbones like someone I used to know.

Anyway, I'm sorry, Dr. Alma. Of course you're really a doctor. I don't even know what got into me. I get this feeling lately — like I can't control my own emotions — like I'm

watching myself have a total meltdown. I swear I didn't
have anger issues as a kid. I'm very sorry.

And I shouldn't have thrown the vase like that.

Or grabbed you and kissed you. . . .

It's just that you look so familiar sometimes . . . and
other times, I don't know why, I get mad when you call me
Thomas.

✧ ✧ ✧

Commissioner Paulie stood in the Marlowe hallway with his arms
crossed, gnawing on a straw he'd used to stir his coffee. Principal
Stevenson stood to the side, chewing his nails and tapping his foot
on the marble floor. Detective Mancuso had sweat stains on his
NYPD standard-issue blues as he rifled through the locker marked
1385.

Thomas was watching and listening from inside an empty biology classroom.

"Believe me, Stevenson, I know how annoying these parents can
be," said the commissioner. "They've been calling Police Plaza all
week." Principal Stevenson nodded as he ate what was left of his
cuticles. The commissioner went on, "But I swear, if I have to personally come down to this ritzy little day care one more time . . ."

Principal Stevenson nodded. "I know, I know. Our students have
never been targeted like this before. I can't make sense of it."

Commissioner Paulie squinted at Principal Stevenson. "Do you
have any idea why Marlowe would be the focus of a crime spree
now? I mean, has anything controversial happened here? Any dis-
agreements or worse-than-usual rivalries, or just the same old crap?"

It seemed to Thomas that Paulie was harboring a grudge against the entire New York upper class for what had happened to him at the Goodman-Brown wedding. Thomas checked his watch. Just five minutes until the period bell, when students would file out of the classrooms and into the hallway. Then he could get a closer look at the locker.

"Nothing comes to mind," said Principal Stevenson. "Marla Harker has always been a bit of trouble. She's run away from home before."

"Don't blame the victim, Stevenson," said the commissioner. "Poor girl could be dead in a ditch somewhere. You've got a serial criminal on your hands. Now, what have you found, Mancuso?"

Detective Mancuso turned from the locker and showed his palms, covered in latex gloves. "Nothing, sir. No sign of correspondence with a boy or girlfriend. Her textbooks are untouched. A few ticket stubs for the Samson Diablo tour . . ."

"Anything else? Anything *relevant*?" said the commissioner.

Mancuso shook his head. "I did find a few pages from her journal. . . . Pretty disturbed cookie."

"Rich kids," said Commissioner Paulie with a slight shake of the head. "Lock this place down, would you? Search the lockers around hers, plus all her friends'. No one gets into their locker before we're done."

The bell rang. Students poured into the hallway from all directions. Thomas pushed open the door and collided with the biology teacher. "Oomph!" said the teacher, taking the majority of the blow in his sternum.

"Sorry!" said Thomas as he ran past. "I was just getting an . . . um, my textbook."

The teacher was still doubled over and didn't bother to pursue him. Thomas was tall enough to see the principal directing kids around the pile of books on the floor in front of Marla's locker as Detective Mancuso hurried to shove everything back in. Thomas weaved through the crowd, avoiding eye contact with anyone who might want to stop and talk to him. As he approached Marla's locker, he heard Commissioner Paulie say, "Hurry up, Mancuso!"

Mancuso shoved the rest of the books into the locker and slammed it shut. A few sheets of paper escaped and fluttered to the ground. Thomas loitered nearby, waiting for the three men to clear out. Scary, he thought, that if he became a lawyer, he would be part of the same legal system as these guys.

"What are you doing here?" said a voice over Thomas's shoulder. Thomas whipped around, hoping the motion didn't catch anyone's attention. It was Annie. Not so long ago, the two of them texted so much that Thomas knew exactly where she was at any given time. But a lot had happened since then. Now she was the last person Thomas wanted to see.

"Hey, Annie. What are you doing here?"

"That's what I just asked you," said Annie. She attempted a smile, as though they were having a silly conversation, but to Thomas, it was all a ton of awkward.

"Oh, right. I was just seeing if the investigators came up with anything. You know, 'cause I want to be a lawyer . . . 'cause investigators are like lawyers. . . ."

Thomas tried to stem the flow of stupid words. Annie looked at the three men as they marched down the hall. The tide of students filled the open space in front of Marla's locker, and everything was back to normal. Sort of.

"Do they think it's related to Roger?"

"Yeah, I think I heard them say it was the same criminal," said Thomas. He was intending to investigate on his own, but obviously, he had to deal with Annie first. "Listen, Annie, thanks for finding me. I missed you yesterday."

Annie leaned past Thomas to look at the locker. "What do you mean, 'yesterday'?" she said. "And how could they possibly know if it was the same criminal?"

"We didn't hang out yesterday. I was just saying I missed you."

"Thomas, we haven't *hung out* all week. You've been avoiding me. Did those papers fall out of Marla's locker?"

Thomas took a sideways step to block Annie's path. Then he realized how guilty that made him look. Annie stepped around and picked up a crumpled piece of paper. It had been ripped out of a notebook. When she smoothed it out and got a glimpse of the writing, she gasped.

"What?" said Thomas, grabbing the paper. Thomas immediately recognized his own handwriting. It was a page from his journal, a recent page, covered in his own semi-incoherent ramblings. It was a stream of curse words directed at therapists in general, escape plans from New York, and claims that "witches and demons" were out to get him. He had scrawled diagonally across the horizontal text, *Hyde is sick.*

It didn't make any sense. Then again, most of his thoughts didn't make sense anymore. He looked up from the paper, thinking,

It doesn't prove anything. There weren't any obvious links to him. Only someone who had seen his journal, or his handwriting, could possibly guess. Someone like Annie.

Annie just stared at him. The hallway was starting to clear out as students shuffled into class. Annie still hadn't said anything. Thomas was frozen, trying to read suspicion in her face. If he started to act weird now, she might suspect him — whether or not she recognized the page. He had to act normal. *What's the normal way to act in this situation?*

"Oh, hey, look at that," he said. "The writer calls himself Edward a couple times."

"What?" said Annie, peering at the jagged scrawl.

"Yeah, right here," said Thomas. "I guess Marla was working on a persona poem, or maybe it's some townie she's dating."

"What's a townie?" said Annie.

"You know, people who don't go to Marlowe. They just live in town."

"You mean New York City?"

"Yeah," said Thomas, sweating. "Listen, I gotta go. But do you want me to drive you to the hospital after school, to visit Roger?"

Annie adjusted the strap of her purse on her shoulder. "No," she said. "You never liked Roger anyway. No reason to pose now."

"What do mean?" said Thomas, burping out a few awkward laughs. "I liked the guy just fine. I mean, I never *dis*liked him. Besides, I wanted to hang with you."

"Whatever, Thomas," said Annie. "Let's just not worry about hanging out till all this is over. I've got Roger, and film club, and finals. And you haven't even mentioned the debate tournament."

"Oh, right," said Thomas.

The truth was that he hadn't even thought of debate recently. And what was more, it sounded like Annie was dumping him. She leaned over and kissed him on the cheek.

"Take care of yourself. You're sort of coming apart."

"Are you breaking up with me?" said Thomas.

Annie tried a half smile, but it didn't take. "I think you've been breaking up with me for weeks now. I'm just going along with it."

She turned and walked down the hall. A part of Thomas felt like it was dragging behind her. He had already promised himself that after this was over, he would find a way to make it up to Annie. For now, it was probably the safest thing for her to be as far from him as possible.

Unless she knows it was us. She's probably running off right now to tell the cops.

Thomas couldn't deny the voice inside his head. The voice of Edward. Annie was the only person who could put all the pieces together.

Then the answer is simple. Annie's gotta go.

116

BROTHER FROM ANOTHER MOTHER

"Have you ever seen an addict try to quit cold turkey, Thomas?"

"Look, Dr. Alma, I'm not addicted to W. I know addicted people say they're not addicted, but not-addicted people say it, too, sooo . . . You're looking at me like you don't believe me. I've only taken it for a couple weeks. I'm not some junkie."

"Do you have feelings toward junkies?"

"What, like romantic feelings?"

"Feelings in general."

"I don't know what we're talking about. I neither love nor hate nor anything junkies."

"So the answer is that you don't have feelings for them."

"Are you implying that W has made me callous? Like I'm some disaffected American youth murder machine? I've lost touch with humanity?"

"Is that your impression of the situation?"

"I just asked you if that was your impression. I don't wanna be rude or anything, but this feels more like a cross-examination than a counseling session."

"What makes you feel that way?"

"That! The interrogation thing. I asked if you knew how I could quit W, and you're dodging me."

"What did I say?"

"You said, have I ever seen a junkie quit cold turkey."

"Well?"

"I saw some movie where the guy gets lockjaw and spasms, then breaks an arm falling out a window. . . . Huh. I guess that answers my question."

"Mmm-hmm. I suggest you be discreet, of course. Just finish the bottle gradually, and after that, no more."

"Excuse me. Everyone? Is this thing on? *Excuse* me! Hi. As you all know, my name is Lucy Spencer and I'm the student council president. . . . What? Fine, I'm the *interim outgoing incumbent* student council president. Thank you, Charlotte. Anyway, welcome, everyone, to the annual Marlowe Academy Fund-Raiser and Pancake Social for Eliminating the Homeless!"

As Thomas entered the circus tent in Central Park's great lawn, he marveled at the idea of calling this function a pancake social, as though they were sitting on folding chairs in a school gym, with a science teacher flinging all-you-can-eat flapjacks onto paper plates for five bucks a head. Roughly a hundred families were gathered in the banquet area, enjoying a catered meal of blinis and caviar. Industrial heaters shaped like umbrella stands fought off the November chill but didn't sit so close as to melt the crème fraîche. A legion of waiters carried mimosas to parents with the same urgency as medics in battlefield trenches. This was the Marlowe PTA.

A few parents had already adjourned to a corner of the space that functioned as the smoking room, with high-back leather chairs and a selection of Cuban cigars and Kentucky bourbon.

Lucy outdid herself, thought Thomas as he passed several carnival games decorated with autumnal harvest themes. Of course, the police commissioner had also outdone himself, sending a cop to attend the breakfast. For all Thomas knew, there could have been half a dozen nonuniformed detectives inside the tents as well. If Thomas caused a scene, he knew the police would be all over him with questions.

Connor stood at a shooting gallery with a group of sophomore girls, firing a BB gun at iron cutouts of birds painted like the catalog of the Audubon Society. Black-billed gulls, mallards of the American Northwest, even a puffin — each worth five tickets. Every time he won, Connor handed a stuffed animal to one of the squealing entourage and got a peck on the cheek in return. Several parents were standing nearby, telling the event coordinator that a "murder simulator" was not appropriate at a Marlowe function. "Are there *any* games here that help with SAT prep?" said one concerned mother.

"What if there was a carnival game that rewarded empathy?" said another. "Wouldn't that be delightful?"

Thomas gave Connor a nod as he passed, heading straight toward the tables. His dad was actually attending something for the first time this semester. Thomas had gotten the e-mail late last night: *Hey, bud. N & I want to attend the pancake thing w/ you. Dress nice. We're meeting her son.*

Pathetic. They used to do everything together. Thomas even had a cubicle at the bank for when he joined his dad on Saturdays at the office. Now their conversations had become hastily written one-liners on their phones. Thomas had written back with something even more brief: *Fine.*

But even so, Thomas couldn't deny that he was excited to see his dad outside the house, where maybe they could have a second of privacy. It had been only a short time since she had moved in, but already their home felt like Vileroy's personal lair. She seemed to know everything that happened there.

And now the existence of a stepbrother had Thomas obsessed with investigating the rest of Vileroy's past — whether she was some kind of magic ghoulish cougar or a con artist gold digger. If he could prove either one, he'd have his life back. He could go back to worrying about debate, and SATs, and scoring an internship at a law firm. All the stuff that used to feel like work. He missed the golf games and pep rallies, and being the best at something. He even missed problem sets in AP physics.

On the promise of that alone, Thomas hadn't taken a single W pill for two days.

Besides, ever since he'd spoken to John, Thomas had finally started to piece together some more of the puzzle. Something had caused his ex-girlfriend Belle's face to change. Thomas's face had also changed. John had claimed that the W contained bonedust . . . a fountain of youth. Last year, he had met somebody who seemed a lot older than her face: Bicé Faust. Belle's twin sister. Another kid raised by his new stepmother.

All roads seemed to lead back to Madame Vileroy, the creepy woman who now lived in his own house and slept just a few doors from his room.

If only he had managed to get into Vileroy's old apartment that day or even gathered some clues in the lobby. He remembered a shadow in the window, dark corridors leading up into the apartment, a childish voice, a familiar face, and then a blow to the head. Who was living there? The lost Faust kids? Someone else? Only people who had once lived with Vileroy could give him the information he needed, so Thomas had spent most of his time trying to figure out where they were. So far, nothing. He called their school in Geneva, but it had no record of five new students from New York.

Thomas spotted his dad — or rather, he spotted the usual crowd of parents orbiting his table — near the multiethnic ice sculptures of Native Americans enjoying an embarrasingly modern Thanksgiving meal. Thomas passed by several parents lecturing the hired sculptor on the similarities of using colored ice to using blackface. "I just don't understand what it's supposed to mean," said one concerned father. "Are you saying that the natural state of ice is whiteness?"

"I think it's saying that Natives are cold-blooded."

"Don't call them 'Natives,' dear."

"Really? I thought they preferred to be called that."

"Don't call them 'they,' dear."

"I hope I haven't offended anyone. I really do think everyone is equal."

Thomas approached his dad's table. As the people surrounding it jostled for position, a sliver of space opened up, and Thomas glimpsed Madame Vileroy sitting beside his dad. Oddly, she was staring right back at him, as though she were anticipating the split second that a few stray elbows would clear their line of sight. Her jackal smile was waiting for him. Her branded eye seemed to see everything — to know everything.

At that moment, Thomas felt a presence fighting for grip on his mind, like a claw scraping across his brain. The pain almost knocked him over. Thomas grabbed his head. His knees almost buckled. He could hear something happening inside — as though he were being pushed out of his own mind — or at least pushed to the back. Thomas could feel his eyes roll back. He was vaguely aware of the cop patrolling around, but his thought was interrupted by a grating voice:

One frigging cop? If he touches us, we put a salad fork in his ear.

Thomas didn't bother looking around for the owner of the voice. He knew it was inside him. It was almost as familiar as his own. And as Thomas weaved through the crowd to his dad's table, the voice was fighting for control.

"Thomas!" said Mr. Goodman-Brown, ignoring everyone but his son. "Thomas, I saved you a seat." His dad got up to hug him, but Thomas sank right through the man's arms into the chair. Mr. Goodman-Brown ended up awkwardly hugging Thomas's shoulders. "You all right?" said his father.

"Yeah," said Thomas, "I just have a headache."

A waiter placed a champagne flute full of orange juice in front of Thomas. His dad said to the waiter, "Do you have any aspirin in the back?"

122

"No!" said Thomas. "No pills." But the waiter had scuttled off already. "I'm fine," added Thomas. He wasn't fine. He was losing grip on his own mind. He could feel his vision separating from his eyes — as though someone were pulling him away from binoculars. "I think I got food poisoning."

"From Orin's food?" said his dad. "He's usually so careful."

"No. Uh. It wasn't Orin," said Thomas. He was having trouble just sitting upright. Now he had to defend their personal chef. "Orin's great. I got some late-night sashimi."

"Oh, Thomas," said Mr. Goodman-Brown. "You could have just woken Orin—"

Thomas clanked his champagne flute down on the table hard enough to spill some juice. "Geez, Dad, can I just have some diarrhea without you crawling up there to investigate? Let's move along."

The crowd of nearby adults acted as if a waiter had dropped an entire tray. The only sounds were the distant hum of the generators from the kitchen tent and the buzz of the industrial heaters.

Mr. Goodman-Brown calmly dabbed his napkin on his lips and set it back on his lap. *Might have gone too far,* thought Thomas. His dad didn't seem intimidated by the silence. He waited till the crowd slowly resumed conversation. Thomas glanced at Nicola. As always, she looked right through him.

"Thomas," said Mr. Goodman-Brown in a slow, deliberate voice, "if you need to take a minute to calm down, then feel free. But today is a big day for our family, and I'd appreciate it if you'd drop the attitude by the time Eddie — Edward — your stepbrother arrives."

Edward. Thomas felt a wave of nausea. He slouched in his seat. He didn't have the energy to try to figure out the connection. And was his dad *always* this patient and understanding? Thomas had expected the man to snap off the stem of a champagne flute and lunge at him. Instead, his dad stayed as monotone and nonconfrontational as Dr. Alma. And somehow that made Thomas furious. Ever since he'd married Vileroy, Mr. Goodman-Brown had changed into some kind of Stepford Dude.

So condescending, he thought as a slow rage began to creep from his chest all the way to his hands and feet. His fingers curled around the edge of the table to flip the entire thing over in an explosive clatter.

The voice in his head grew louder. ***Old-money, horny, sad mortal prick thinks he can treat me like a kid? I'll eat his eyeballs like they were Jell-O shots.***

Thomas was losing control. He had the fuzzy sensation that his muscles were tense and ready to pounce. What scared him wasn't that he was about to attack his dad but that he could barely feel his own muscles. Thomas turned his focus toward his fingers, gripping the edge of the table. *Let go,* he thought.

He heard a whisper in his own mind. ***No.***

His dad kept talking, but Thomas could hear him only from a distance. "I don't expect you to like him, Thomas, but Nicola and I are hoping you can at least be civil."

Civil? mused the voice in Thomas's mind. ***I'm gonna cut that skin between your fingers with a bread knife.***

"I have to get out of here," said Thomas. He focused all his energy once again on peeling each finger away from the table.

"Thomas—" said Mr. Goodman-Brown, but Vileroy put a hand on his elbow.

124

"Let him go, dear. He needs some time to sort himself before Edward arrives."

Edward, Edward, Edward. The name made his head hurt.

Mr. Goodman-Brown reached over to hold her hand while Thomas stumbled away from the table. As he grasped for purchase on his own mind, Thomas weaved through the crowd. He thought he heard Connor shout, "Hey, T. Get over here," but Thomas's vision was too blurry to see where his friend was. He couldn't exactly remember the last time he took a hit of W—but the symptoms were the same. Except this time they were lasting a lot longer. His hand moved involuntarily to his pocket, to make sure the bottle was secure.

Over the loudspeaker, Lucy Spencer said, "Everyone? Everyone. We'll be starting the games soon. So please finish that last blini and clear the tables for the first round of the team sudoku challenge!"

Thomas leaned on a bar table, waiting for a dizzy spell to pass. The cop had noticed him acting strange, and he was staring. The voice in Thomas's mind said, **You know, you're pretty strong, Tommy. I like that.**

"Leave me alone," said Thomas.

Over his shoulder, Thomas heard a slight gasp. He turned. It was Annie.

"Sorry," she said. "I didn't know you could see me."

"I couldn't," said Thomas. "Or, I mean, I wasn't talking to you."

Annie seemed equally hurt by Thomas's explanation. "I mean, I was just rehearsing something I wanna tell somebody . . . not you."

"I do that sometimes," said Annie.

She rocked back and forth on her heels. Thomas tried to think of another subject to talk about—something other than Roger's assault,

Marla's disappearance, or the police investigation. The truth was that they didn't have very much to talk about. In fact, if he wanted to spare her more pain, he knew he would have to keep her at arm's length.

You're such a Debbie Downer. I'll take great care of her.

Thomas's muscles tensed. Edward was quickly taking control. Thomas sighed. "Listen, Annie. I don't want to be weird about this."

Annie had been looking in every direction but Thomas's. Now she looked him in the eye. With everything going on, Thomas couldn't tell if he had any feelings for her, but he knew he didn't want to be alone. *You mean, you don't want to be alone with* me.

Maybe it was selfish. He said, "We've both had a lot going on. I hope we're still . . ."

As boring as a nun's panty drawer? Yes, you are.

Thomas stammered to finish his thought with Edward interrupting constantly. Thankfully, Annie stepped in. "Are you asking if we can still be friends?"

"Yes."

"Yes," said Annie.

"Good," said Thomas.

When are you gonna wise up and dump this thing?

"I should go," blurted Thomas. He felt Edward's thoughts forming in his mouth. Annie looked surprised. But it was better to seem crazy than to let Edward talk to her.

"Really?" said Annie. "I thought we could sit together."

Yeah, let's play sudoku, you sad waste of young skin.

"Maybe a rain check?" said Thomas. "What are you doing tomorrow night?"

The transformation had already begun. Thomas caught his

126

reflection in the espresso machine in the corner of the bar. His hair was growing longer, darker, his eyes becoming almost almond shaped. Annie would notice any second.

"I'm having dinner with my family," she said. "Maybe—"

"Could I join you?" interrupted Thomas. "I'll bring some wine from my dad's cellar."

Thomas had to look away. His skin was becoming pale. The muscles in his shoulders were growing to double their size.

"I can ask if it'd be OK," said Annie. "But yeah, definitely."

"Great," said Thomas. He kissed her on the cheek and shouldered past her before Annie could turn around. Thomas ran to the entrance of the tent. As he ducked out, he looked over his shoulder and saw Detective Mancuso staring right at him, speaking into the walkie-talkie on his shoulder harness. Thomas scrambled toward the food tent.

The makeshift kitchen was in full-scale production, with an army of line cooks calling instructions to one another. No one noticed Thomas huddled in the corner by an industrial fridge. Thomas unbuttoned his shirt and took it off just in time, before his growing frame tore the fabric. He had an undershirt on underneath that stretched with his upper body. His new frame was hulking, but Edward's body was definitely more muscular. Thomas was a natural swimmer. Edward seemed like an unnatural baseball player—juiced up to have the perfect torso.

Thomas crouched beside the fridge, grinding his teeth from the pain, watching the last of his features changing in the hazy reflection on the stainless-steel panel of the fridge. He had no idea how this was happening without having taken any W.

I'm just tired of letting you drive.

"No," groaned Thomas. Every nerve in his brain was snapping like a rubber band.

Suck it, Toy Scout.

Edward crumpled up the shirt and stuffed it behind the fridge. He waited for a cook to pass by before standing up and leaving the tent. As he walked back into the main tent, two police officers hustled past him. "I've lost visual," said one officer.

"Probably throwing up in the bushes somewhere. I'm telling you, Mancuso, the kid looked hungover."

—※—

"Everyone, put your pens down. I see you, Mr. Wirth. Pens down. I mean it. OK, did any team finish the entire puzzle?"

Annie was still standing by the banquet tables, glancing occasionally at the entrance, probably waiting for Thomas to return. She looked self-conscious, hanging out all alone. She had her phone in her hand, checking it a bit too frequently.

Thomas expected her to look up and smile, the way she always did when she saw him walking in. But when they made eye contact, Annie didn't seem to recognize him.

He looked like Edward now. Thomas wasn't in control.

Thomas was forced to watch as Edward sauntered forward. Annie looked back down at her phone. As Edward passed her, he bumped her shoulder a little.

Don't, thought Thomas—now he was the other voice, the silenced half, and he could feel the frustration of it. Edward was just doing this to mess with him.

Annie glanced up. "Sorry," she said. Seeing her as a stranger, Thomas was suddenly struck by details he had long taken for granted. Her bangs, sweeping across her forehead and behind her ear. The tiny birthmark behind her earlobe. The near-invisible hairs on her neck that were standing up as Edward continued to stare at her.

Annie looked up again. She gave a nervous smile. "Do I know you?"

Edward just grinned at her and let the silence go stale before he finally said, "No, you don't."

He walked off, gliding through the crowd toward his mother's table. The Marlowe girls standing with Connor stopped in mid-conversation to gawk at Edward's chiseled bare arms. The undershirt hugged his pecs and six-pack like Cling Wrap — not exactly the Marlowe uniform. Edward nodded to a few of the girls and some of the moms but didn't stop to talk.

This never happened before, thought Thomas.

That's because I'm better-looking than you.

But that wasn't what Thomas was referring to. Every other time, the W had given him some aspect of what he now knew were Edward's emotions — his excitement, his sadness, his charm; each pill was a different piece of a new *other* self — then knocked him out. It was like watching a dream — or reliving a memory — of his time as Edward, all to the beat of the flashing lights of Club Elixir. But this time, W wasn't the cause. He hadn't taken any. Could it still be in his system? Thomas was awake, inside his own brain, fully aware of what he was doing but unable to change any of it.

Is this how Edward feels when I'm in control? Is he watching me from the inside?

Suddenly, Thomas feared that the W had had some lasting effect on his mind. Or worse, that this Edward was far more than a persona but someone else entirely, possessing him. John said the bonedust was a source of immortality. Maybe instead of giving him long life, the W had given him a second life.

Welcome to the movie, Tommy. It's almost time for the credits.

They had reached the table. Madame Vileroy stood up and crooned, as any mother would.

"Edward," she said. "I haven't seen you in far too long, my darling."

She seemed to float around the table—never a clumsy step or an awkward pause to push her chair back—perfect frictionless motion. As she kissed Edward on each cheek, she whispered in his ear, "Hello in there, Thomas."

Thomas would have screamed if he'd had any vocal cords to scream with.

Of course she knows, he thought. *Of course Edward is her son.* After what John had told him about W, and after what he'd seen happen to Belle last year, he shouldn't have been surprised by any of this.

Mr. Goodman-Brown took his cue from Nicola and stood.

"This is my Charles," said Vileroy. Even in his position, Thomas caught the fleeting wrinkle on his dad's forehead when he was referred to as hers.

Creepy, thought Thomas.

"It's nice to meet you," said Mr. Goodman-Brown, extending his hand. Edward took it and squeezed hard. Thomas caught on to the idea. He thought, *I wouldn't do that.* With uncanny timing, Mr. Goodman-Brown reacted to the tightening grip and clamped down on Edward's hand. Explosions of pain and expletives flashed through Edward's thoughts. For a second, Thomas was proud. *Dad used to row crew. And he's in finance. He puts up with these alpha male monkey power games all the time.*

Mr. Goodman-Brown peered deep into Edward's eyes but didn't betray his feelings in any way. For the first time, Thomas knew why everyone said his dad was so good at negotiating. Thomas could feel the bones crushing in his palm.

Wait! thought Thomas. *I could feel that.*

Edward was losing his concentration. His hold on their body was weakening. Suddenly, every sense returned to Thomas. The smell of apple-smoked bacon and Kona coffee. Marlowe parents discussing their winter getaway plans to Shanghai. Lucy Spencer speaking into the mic: "Did anyone complete seven rows of the sudoku?"

Thomas was back. And his dad was crushing his hand.

You angsty little piece of upper-crust sperm. I will kill you from the inside. I will take you over and ruin you.

Thomas ignored Edward's rage wail. He knew his own face and body would return soon — right in front of everyone.

"Why don't you take a seat," said Mr. Goodman-Brown. "My son, Thomas, should be back any minute."

"Yes," said Nicola. "In fact, I've texted him just now, to let him know we're all here." She smiled and held up her phone as a visual aid. It was immediately accompanied by the ringtone, blaring from Thomas's pocket. Thomas clasped his hand over his jeans and pressed frantically at the SILENCE button through the fabric. His dad noticed and raised an eyebrow.

"I should go, actually," said Thomas. His hair was starting to recede.

"Not you, too," said Mr. Goodman-Brown, settling back in his seat. "Why is it so hard to feed you boys caviar in a room full of pretty girls?"

"I dunno," said Thomas. His voice cracked. "It's probably the airport calling. They, uh, lost my luggage." He put his hand over his face and raced to get back out of the tent hall. *Why would Vileroy even do that?* thought Thomas. *It doesn't help her in any way to expose this.*

Just for the hell of it, Tommy. The amusing little piece of everyday hell.

Thomas almost knocked over a tray table as he scrambled out. He ran through the tent curtain, face-first into the chest of Detective Mancuso. Thomas stumbled backward. Mancuso expelled a gust of air.

"Sorry," said Thomas. He tried to sidestep and continue on, but the officer caught him by the arm. "Hold on a minute, son."

Wanna show him a magic trick, Thomas?

Thomas didn't need to be reminded that any second now his face and body would begin contorting back into their original shape.

"You seen a kid around here a little shorter than you, acting kind of weird?" asked Detective Mancuso. Thomas didn't have time for this.

"This is Marlowe," he said.

He tried to pull his arm away, but Mancuso tightened his grasp. "What does that mean?" said the detective.

"It means that half these kids eat medication like it's Skittles, and the other half just act weird."

132

Thomas wrenched his arm away and walked into the kitchen tent. Detective Mancuso shook his head. "I hate this case," he grumbled as he walked back to the bar. Thomas made it to his corner by the refrigerator just in time to change back. The pain was so sharp that it left lingering aftershocks, similar to waking up after a night at Elixir.

He was halfway through this little charade. Now all he had to do was go back and pretend that something came up or that he wasn't feeling well. He reached behind the fridge and pulled out his shirt. He used the reflection to fix his hair, then ducked out of the kitchen.

It took so much concentration to hold off Edward. Thomas was shaking with the exertion. Oddly, all he wanted to do was take a W and sleep through everything rather than keep fighting every step of the way.

Why don't you? thought Edward in the gentlest tone he'd used yet. Thomas's hand brushed against his pocket. The bottle rattled as he walked across the room.

"Hi, Thomas!"

Thomas looked up. It was Annie again. Thomas breathed a curse. "Hey, Annie. I just forgot to get something from my dad." He didn't stop walking.

"Oh," said Annie. "I checked with my mom and she'd love to have you over for dinner."

"Great!" said Thomas. "It's a date, then."

"OK!" said Annie. She had to shout. Thomas was long gone.

"Congratulations!" said Lucy Spencer. "Mr. Wirth at table twelve wins for finishing five rows of the puzzle!"

Thomas didn't have much time. He balled his hand into a fist and kept moving.

"Thomas," said Mr. Goodman-Brown, "you just missed Edward."

Thomas slunk into his seat and let his dad clap him on the shoulder. "Oh, yeah?" said Thomas. "Is he still around?"

Nicola Vileroy gave a knowing smile. She seemed impressed with his acting.

"He's taking a call," she said.

"I saw your friend Annie," said Mr. Goodman-Brown.

Thomas was distracted, drumming his fingers on the table. "Huh?"

"I saw your friend," said his dad. "You should ask her to join us."

"No," said Thomas.

"How is she holding up?" said Madame Vileroy.

Thomas stopped drumming on the table. "What do you mean?" Thomas knew he was falling into another of her traps. But he couldn't do anything about it.

"Her friend is still in the hospital."

"Oh, that's right," said Mr. Goodman-Brown. "And that other girl. Have they been updating you guys on that case?"

"No, Dad," said Thomas. "It's police business."

"But you're safe? At school, they have security?"

"Yes, Dad."

The mention of security made Thomas look around for Detective Mancuso at the bar. As soon as he turned around, it seemed, the officer glanced over. They made eye contact. Thomas whipped back around.

He's coming this way, Thomas.

"Thomas, are you OK?" said Nicola.

He was losing his grip again. Edward was pulling him back. His shirt felt tighter. Thomas reached for his glass of orange juice but knocked it over instead.

"Darn it!" said Thomas.

"It's all right," said his dad. "We'll get you another one."

"Feeling dizzy," said Nicola. Thomas couldn't tell if it was a question or a command. The transformation was coming on even faster than last time. Thomas caught the slightest glint in the branded eye of Vileroy.

"I'm feeling dizzy," said Thomas.

No kidding.

Mr. Goodman-Brown turned in his seat. "Excuse me," he said to a nearby waiter, but Thomas interrupted.

"Don't worry about it. I'll refill it myself."

Thomas grabbed the glass and lurched toward the nearby buffet table. Even though there were pitchers of juice at both ends of the table, Thomas headed into the crowd, where parents were still debating the sociopolitical merits of the Native American ice sculpture. He squeezed through, hoping his dad and Detective Mancuso had lost the line of sight as he went around the back and crawled under the table.

As he ripped his shirt off and suppressed a grunt of pain, he heard his dad's voice. "Thomas? Where'd you go?"

Thomas had seconds before he was again at the mercy of his other self, Vileroy's own son. Now he was certain that she was responsible for Edward's presence, just as she had been responsible for Belle's face changing. If his suspicions were correct, that it was the W that had opened his mind to Edward, then she must have had something to do with the pills, too, with Nikki from Elixir, and even John Darling's bonedust, since it had the same healing effect as W. The thought occurred to him that maybe Vileroy had something to do with Roger's attack and Marla's disappearance — or even the missing school nurse.

He pulled out his phone and texted as fast as he could. *Sorry G2G. Sick.*

At the last second, Thomas pressed SEND.

I win, thought Thomas as he floated back into the abyss of unconsciousness.

"Edward!" said Mr. Goodman-Brown as he approached the buffet table a minute or two later. "Stay right there. Thomas should be around here somewhere."

"I doubt it," said Edward.

"Hold on a sec," said Mr. Goodman-Brown. "This might be him." He pulled out his phone and read the text. "Huh," said Mr. Goodman-Brown. "I guess he went home. Now, what were you saying, Edward?"

"Don't worry about it."

Edward had better things to do than glad-hand Nicola's latest chew toy. As he walked out of the tent, anonymously past Detective Mancuso, he thought, **No, Tommy. There are a lot of ways this can end, but you don't win in any of them.**

Edward pulled out Thomas's phone and began typing another text, this time to Annie: *Can't do dinner. Lata — tgb.*

THE LONGBORNS

London, England, in the Year of Our Lord 1536

> *Dear Richard,*
>
> *I write to make an urgent request of you. I know that I have been wicked and that in our tutorial days I made you do terrible, depraved things. But you must forget all that, because my life is in the gravest danger. I sense an evil rising up within me. It has been bubbling there for all my sixteen years and threatens to spill over. Sometimes I want to embrace it. . . . I know that it will end me. And if it doesn't, this will: Mother has been whispering strange things. She says that I am not destined to live out my youth in this world, that I must rather embrace a greater destiny. She has been watching me as I sleep. Last night, I heard her gathering up the last of her beauty dust — you know what I refer to — and I think she means to kill me to make more of it. You may think me crazy, but a few nights ago she tried to say good-bye, in her twisted way. She said that I, Edward*

Hyde, will live out the ages among kings and Caesars and that I will come back again, in the far-off future, as heir to great empires, cleansed of any human pity or conscience.

Then yesterday, I thought I dreamed that she cut off one of my toes and ground it into fine powder. I wouldn't have thought much of it, except that I woke up with my foot bandaged and sore and my bed bloodied. What else can all this signify but that she has gone mad and means to butcher me in ritual? I pray you to find my father, as I must have one. I fear my time has come, for I hear her footsteps now. . . .

Your wretched friend,
Edward Hyde

London, England, 1886

My dear Dr. Jekyll,

I must be brief, as I am at this very moment pursued by police and others who will do me harm. I wish you to know that I am well hidden and that you need labour under no alarm for my safety, as I have means of escape on which I place a sure dependence. You have been a faithful benefactor, whom I have so long unworthily repaid for a thousand generosities. Of all my friends past and present, you have been the most magnanimous. I wish the authorities to make no connection between us, for I am moving onward.

I leave this letter in the capable hands of your maid-servant.

Your grateful friend,
Edward Hyde

New York, NY, present day

Dear Thomas,

I got rid of Annie for you. I write this in our journal so you don't mess it up with your stupid-ass attempts at making things right. Of all the benefactors I've had over the centuries, you're the biggest bumbling idiot. But I'll tell you one thing: I like New York. I like Mother's new house. I'm not going anywhere. It's you and me forever, bitch. . . .

Your pissed-off friend,
Edward Hyde

The next evening, Thomas spent an hour searching for his journal. He figured he'd crank out his obligatory four hundred words for Dr. Alma before going to dinner at Annie's, but lately, he kept misplacing everything—his journal, his phone, his keys. He really needed the journal now, though. He wanted to see the place where the page from Marla's locker had been ripped out. Could the page really have come from his journal? He knew it had, but he wanted to check anyway. Besides, he wanted to write down his thoughts about John's bonedust and his bottle of W, which was probably the thing that changed his face and his thoughts, opening his innermost parts to Edward. What was the connection between the two? W came from Nikki, maybe somehow from Nicola, considering that she claimed Edward as her own son. And according to John Darling, bonedust came from the old RA and the missing school nurse. He should search for them online.

Later . . .

By the time he gave up the journal search, it was already seven p.m. and time to head out. Thomas knew that tonight was important to Annie. It would be the first time they'd met up since getting back together at the pancake social yesterday. He wondered if he should put on cologne. Or maybe wear a suit. *No*, he thought. Better play it casual. He grabbed a light jacket off his bed and started to head out. Then, halfway out the door, he turned back toward the closet, stuffed a blue tie into his pocket (just in case), and hurried down the stairs and out to the foyer elevator.

Annie lived on the Upper West Side, just across the park from Thomas, so Thomas decided to walk. Central Park in late autumn is a place straight out of the movies. Thomas used to go jogging there with his mom when he was a kid. She'd jog in place while he caught up, or run really slowly and pretend to be amazed by her "super athlete" son. Meanwhile, he would be hauling it just to prove that he could beat her. Was he ten years old then? Eleven? If she were alive now, Thomas would probably have to slow down so she could keep up. As he strolled through the lush orange-and-brown trees lining the footpath through the center of the park, Thomas thought of Thanksgiving and Christmas and how if his mom were around instead of Madame Vileroy, she would already be reserving turkeys and counting place settings.

As he was passing a row of artists displaying their wares, Thomas felt something skip. It was bizarre. He was looking at a guy spray painting a red planet on a piece of cardboard, and then suddenly he wasn't. He was three artists down from that guy, who was suddenly finished with his picture and selling it to a guy with a paunch who wasn't there before. Edward whispered in his head.

Don't do it, Thomas. Don't drag her back into it.

He rubbed his head and kept walking. He had to do something about this. Edward appeared in his mind so often now that he thought maybe the W had done permanent damage. "Shut up!" he said out loud. A woman pushing a stroller turned, then sped up.

I got rid of her the easy way. Don't make me kill her.

"Shut up. Shut up. Shut up," he whispered, and power walked all the way to Annie's house. Edward's thoughts made no sense. Who was he talking about? Annie? Couldn't be, since no one had "gotten rid" of her. Marla? Oh, God, Marla. The thought of her, of that night they spent together and her disappearance the morning after, made him feel queasy. Did he have something to do with her disappearance? Was she locked up in some basement somewhere, trying to breathe through a bloody gag? What about Roger? Could he feel and think in his coma? No matter how hard he tried, Thomas couldn't remember laying a hand on him. But Marla seemed so sure that he did it, and then she vanished.

He arrived at Annie's building and ran up the stairs to burn off some steam. She only lived on the seventh floor. He knocked on the door and waited, tapping his foot like a preteen on a first date.

Time to head home now. I'm warning you, Thomas.

Go away, Edward. . . .

He caught himself. Why the hell was he on a first-name basis with Vileroy's evil body-snatching son, anyway? He straightened his collar and knocked again. Two voices were speaking behind the door. One of them laughed, then the door swung open. Annie's mother stood there wearing jeans and a Dartmouth T-shirt, her nose covered in flour.

"Um, T-t-homas," she stammered. "Hi there." Thomas had rarely seen Mrs. Longborn flustered like this. She was one of those people who never had a bad day. She was petite, like Annie, with long curly brown hair and a button nose that she crinkled when she was thinking of what to say. She had started her own handbag company that was later bought by a big-name designer. Now she spent her days being supermom. Annie was the only one at school who brought her lunches from home, usually some Moroccan or Indian experimental dish her mom packed for her.

He said hello and waited to be invited in, but Annie's mom looked confused. She was chewing the inside of her cheek and rubbing the tip of her nose with purple-stained hands. "We weren't expecting you," she said.

"Sorry?" said Thomas. "I . . . Annie invited me for dinner."

There was another pause and Mrs. Longborn glanced back into the house, then she whispered, "But honey, you canceled."

Thomas just stood there, looking at his own stupid expression in the shiny glass of the hallway mirror, unable to remember what Mrs. Longborn was talking about.

"Sweetie, are you OK?" she said, putting a hand on his shoulder.

Then Annie appeared at the door, fancy sketching pencils firmly planted in her hair. She, too, was wearing old jeans and had purple stuff all over her hands. "Thomas!" She didn't look happy to see him at all. She crossed her arms and hung back from the door while her mom glanced back and forth between the two of them.

"Look, why don't you join us, then?" Mrs. Longborn said finally. She reached inside and took Annie's hand and puller her closer. "We were just making an all-purple dinner to cheer us up. Right?" She looked at Annie with excited eyes.

Annie rolled her eyes and said, "Mom!"

"Sorry, honey, but he's gonna find out soon enough that all the food's purple. Nothing better than playing with food coloring to cure the blues."

"I wasn't blue," said Annie, arms still crossed. "I was perfectly happy. In fact, I was just about to go out with some people from NYU. Excuse me."

Mrs. Longborn laughed and threw her arm around her daughter. "Oh, stop now. Your friend's here. Why can't we share our purple dinner?"

Annie shrugged. "Thought you were too busy," she shot at Thomas.

"Sorry," said Thomas again. "I don't know why . . . I mean, someone must have taken my phone. I don't remember ever —"

"Save it," Annie said, and went back inside. "I've got a roast chicken to dye."

"Super gross," said Mrs. Longborn, and she shut the door behind Thomas. "I call the drumstick!"

Well, now we have to kill 'em both, don't we? I call the mom.

~~~~

Thomas shifted the food around on his plate. It was by far the grossest thing he had ever faced at a dinner table — purple chicken, purple carrots, purple mashed potatoes with Denoix's Purple Condiment. What were these chicks on?

"So, um, you do this often?" he asked. "Dyeing dinner?"

"Why not?" said Mrs. Longborn. She winked at Annie and took a bite of chicken. "It's fun."

"You don't have to stay," said Annie to Thomas. She didn't seem quite so angry anymore, but it was obvious from her fidgeting during the first half of dinner that she was embarrassed to have needed a cheer-up dinner to get over Thomas canceling.

That's right, Thomas. You don't have to stay.

Edward, back off. . . .

Thomas moved some carrots around on his plate. "Look, I'm really sorry. I don't know who sent you that text."

"Sure," she said, and took a bite of a dinner roll that looked more gray than purple.

He figured maybe he should focus on winning over the mom. Annie was nowhere near ready to forgive and play nice.

Who cares about the mom, numb nuts? She's as good as dead.

"The school pancake thing was nice, huh?" said Thomas, trying not to look at what he was putting in his mouth.

"Oh, yes!" said Mrs. Longborn. "I helped organize some of

144

that. I think everyone has been pretty disturbed lately . . . after, you know . . ." She touched Annie's hair. Obviously, they'd spent a lot of time talking about Roger.

"I went to see him today," said Annie. "I just can't figure out who'd do this."

"You don't have to, hon," said Mrs. Longborn. "The police can do that."

"I still have that weird diary page from Marla's locker," said Annie. "I've been Googling articles online on how to analyze handwriting. I tried to get samples of Marla's and all her friends' homework pages from their teachers, but they all said no."

Thomas could feel his heart pounding. His hands felt sweaty, and that queasy feeling came over him again. He gripped his napkin.

I told you this would happen. . . .

"Annie." He swallowed hard. Suddenly he couldn't think of what to say next. He started to say, *Maybe you should leave it to the police.* Then he changed his mind and moved in the direction of *Can I see that paper again?* But when he opened his mouth, what came out was "I'm so sorry about Roger. He's a good guy."

Annie smiled for the first time. "Thanks," she whispered. She started chewing her lips, as if she was embarrassed. "I'm gonna go check on the rice pudding."

Thomas's stomach turned. "Purple rice pudding?"

"Yeah," said Annie excitedly. "It was the first thing we made this morning. We had to do it twice, because the milk kept clumping."

Mrs. Longborn brought a napkin to her lips, and Thomas thought he saw her hiding her laughter behind it. "I'll pass, honey," Annie's mom said. "Calories."

145

"Actually, Annie," said Thomas, "how about we go out for dessert? I was gonna show you this great place I know."

You just don't listen.

—————

In the taxi downtown, Annie took his hand. "Your wrists look swollen," she said, and he pulled his hand away. He rubbed his wrists with his thumbs and noticed that his watch was getting tight, leaving a red mark on his skin.

"I don't know why," he said.

"And you look a lot thinner lately," she said. "And you're acting weird. Have you been OK? You're not still going to Elixir, are you?"

"Nah," said Thomas. He felt a little guilty for playing so innocent, but he had already put Annie through all kinds of crap. "Not since Roger. I'm really sorry about the text. I've just been having a hard time."

Annie nodded and took his hand again. "So where are we going?" she asked cheerfully, as though she was trying to distract him with happy thoughts.

"My favorite place when I was a kid," he said. "In Little Italy."

Annie laughed. "Even I know there's no such thing as Little Italy anymore."

"Just wait."

Ten minutes later, the taxi pulled up in front of an unmarked building on Mulberry Street. Thomas had been texting in the cab, and two minutes after the taxi drove off, the old wooden door squeaked open and a diminutive man in a dirty apron peeked his head out and squinted at the dark street.

"Tomaso! It's you!" he shouted as soon as he saw them. He held out his thick hairy arms and rushed toward them. *"Benvenuto! Benvenuto!* How long is it been?" Thomas let Giorgio slap him on the back about a dozen times before he pulled away.

"Couple months, I guess," said Thomas.

"Your pop go through with that remarriage thing?" asked Giorgio, rolling his eyes, then, spotting Annie, switching to a broad smile and a friendly wink. "Who is this?"

"This is Annie," said Thomas. Giorgio lunged for Annie's hand with both of his and shook with such ferocity that she laughed.

"Welcome to Quattro Formaggi!" he said.

"I thought that restaurant closed last year," said Annie. "I read about some huge local petition to bring it back."

Giorgio nodded several times. "Yes, yes, we close for public. We open for special guest only. Tomaso is family. His mother, God rest her, was the goddaughter to my wife, God rest her, too. Come. Now I cook for you."

"Now?" said Annie. "It's almost eleven."

"Never late for cooking," said Giorgio.

As they followed Giorgio inside, Annie turned to Thomas and mouthed, "Wow!" *This is perfect,* he thought, *the best way to make it up to her.* When he was five or six, Thomas used to come to Quattro Formaggi with his mother. They would come in through the back door, and Giorgio would make Thomas a bowl of spaghetti with massive meatballs. Then his mother would say, "Giorgy, help me. I need fat and sugar!" And he would laugh and make her fried brownies with leftover cake batter.

Thomas had never invited anyone here before. After his mother died, he came alone once or twice, but then stopped altogether when it didn't fill the hole. But he had never considered taking Belle or any of his previous girlfriends.

"What you think of fried brownies?" said Giorgio as he started heating up oil.

"Love them!" said Annie. "Well, actually, I've never had them."

"They're Tomaso's favorite," said Giorgio.

Thomas reached into the fridge for the batter. It was exactly where it had always been. And all through the night, Edward didn't say a word.

13

THE WORST OF TIMES

Journal entry #27

You know what's sad, Dr. Alma? I was thinking I should give to charity. My dad gives a lot already, but I was going to take your advice to stop dwelling on my situation, right? So I was going to give some of my own money. But the first thing I think is that any organization I give to is probably going to spend it on more marketing or on administrative costs. **Hookers for the CEOs.** *It never gets to anyone who needs it. How cynical is that?*

Maybe I should just find a homeless guy and give him a grand. **Dirty hobo would spend it on meth.**

I always thought that maybe those guys on the street talking to themselves were unstable. **Lazy, urine-soaked animals.** *But they could be suffering. Maybe they have what I have. Next time I see one of those people* **parasites** *I should* **crush his skull with my golf cleats and hide the body with Marla** *see if I can help.*

Wait . . . I just read what I wrote. . . . I didn't write all this.

✧ ✧ ✧

Things are getting better, thought Thomas as he sat in the open-air Marlowe courtyard. When was the last time he just sat someplace? The atrium was walled off from the city streets with ivy-covered stone. An arboretum, with cherry trees, a koi pond, and ornate benches, had been donated by the father of a Japanese exchange student. In the corner, the cafeteria had set up a gelato stand.

Thomas used to spend every lunch period here. The stone arches of the entryway seemed so intimidating his freshman year. All the uniformed kids seemed so put together. They hung out in packs from their charter prep schools. But Thomas had spent half of eighth grade mourning his mom and the other half in a Semester at Sea program. His father had insisted. He learned to sail, studied biology in the Galápagos, and spent his free time by himself watching the ocean. He talked to his mother, and the rest of the kids didn't hassle him about it.

When he arrived at Marlowe, it seemed that the sailing might have been a bad call. Everyone already knew everyone else. He was behind in three different subjects, and he felt like a tool in a full uniform. He spent the first few lunches at that same picnic table in the atrium, talking on the phone so he wouldn't have to deal with the social scene. He'd call his dad. His dad would always say, "Hi, buddy! Hold on a sec." Then he'd speak to whoever was in his office at the time: "This is important. Can we resume this meeting in an hour?"

150

They'd talk about sports scores, or the game they'd played the night before, or all the legal wranglings of his dad's business deals. Thomas never mentioned his mom. His dad never asked him how school was going. Until one day, Thomas walked out to the atrium and saw Connor Wirth sitting at the same table. "I heard you're a good swimmer," said Connor. The rest was history. Thomas joined the swim team, his dad went back to having meetings during his lunch hour, and they still met up online in the evenings or else Thomas would eat dinner at his dad's office.

As Thomas opened his laptop and clicked VIDEO CHAT, he took a mental account of everything in his life that was positive. First positive thing: He had quit W. Dr. Alma had said that dwelling on the "negative elements" in his life would become a mild form of neurosis. Thomas had taken a joke from Connor's book and said, "What if my mild neuroticism is wild eroticism? Would that create some kind of tear in the space-time continuum, Doctor?" She didn't even crack a smile. He was embarrassed that he ever said it.

Thomas opened the chat application and clicked on the username Sir-Yachts-Alot.

Second positive thing: He was crazy well prepared for the debate practice next hour. All that time in his room taking it easy after weeks of W-induced hallucinogenic nights out at Elixir had given him plenty of study time. He had read the briefs twice. At least, he thought it was twice. He knew he had read them once, then lost track, then he either read them again or recycled through the memory of reading them. OK, maybe he wasn't totally clear of the W in his system.

The chat window popped open on his screen with a time-lagged shot of his dad. "Hey, buddy. What's up?" said Mr. Goodman-Brown.

Third positive thing: When it came down to it, he was a pretty lucky person. Sure, he had only one parent, but he was a good one.

"Nothing, Dad. Just wanted to say I was sorry that the pancake social didn't go so well." Thomas dragged one of the PDFs of the debate briefings over the chat window so he wouldn't see his dad's face.

Over his earbuds, Thomas heard his dad say, "Don't worry about it. We'll get you and Edward together some other time."

Thomas smiled to himself. "What do you think of him?"

His dad paused. Thomas heard him breathe out through his nose. Then he said, "Tell you the truth, Thomas, he seemed like an arrogant little prick who drinks too much Muscle Milk." Thomas laughed. His dad went on, "But, hey, he's Nicola's problem until he goes to some party college. I already told her that this isn't the Disney Channel, and you're my priority. If Eddie Munster messes with you or your GPA, I'll teach him why rich white fifty-somethings make the best Bond villains."

Fourth positive thing: His dad wasn't completely under Vileroy's thumb, and he had no clue about Thomas's little problem.

Thomas moved the PDF file away from the chat window. His dad was smiling at him. Thomas realized it was the first private conversation they had had since Nicola invaded. The look in his eyes told Thomas that the old man was about to say something corny, like, "I'm proud of you, son." Thomas couldn't get all weepy in the middle of the atrium, so he said, "Was that your banker version of a death threat, Pops?"

His dad shrugged. "Sorry. I'm not gangsta enough, Charles

Thomas Goodman-Brown the Third (nonconsecutive), but I'm sure there's *someone* on the Yale alumni board who could help me get rid of a body. That or I'll just find out which hedge fund he invests in and drive his portfolio into the ground."

The bell rang for passing period.

"I could be the Notorious A.I.G. . . . You know . . . as my street name."

"Sure, Dad. I gotta go. Wanna game later?"

"No problem. I'll just run a Fortune 500 while I wait."

Thomas rolled his eyes and shut the laptop.

As he packed up his gear, Thomas let himself believe that things were definitely looking up. And to top it all off, his date with Annie had somehow — despite every possible factor to the contrary — gone well. For the rest of the night, they had avoided the subjects of crazy Marla's disappearance, Roger's assault, and the police lockdown of Marlowe — pretty much everything that had happened that semester. Debate was a great subject for him. Graphic design was a good one for her. The rest of the night was about good Italian food, the old days, and favorite movies.

It was a pretty little picture, full of pastels and highlights. A few dark corners hinted at "the troubled times," but overall, Thomas figured he had weathered the storm. Now if he stayed the course, et cetera, et cetera, he'd be out on the other side, wondering why he ever took W or attended a silly thing like therapy. If he were a painter, he could have used the anguish to do some work critics could call "raw and visceral." For lawyers, the dark nights of the soul were good only when a criminal slammed the table in the interrogation room and said, "Man, you're just a rich white punk in a thousand-dollar suit." Then he could slam the table, too, or turn over the whole thing, if it wasn't bolted to the floor, and say, "You don't know what I've been through either, and the last time I wore a thousand-dollar suit was at my christening. . . . This one could post bail on a school shooting. Now, sit down."

OK, maybe real life wouldn't be so much like a made-for-TV crime flick. He slung his backpack over his shoulder.

That's a cute imagination you have, Tommy.

Thomas fell back onto the bench and grabbed his temples. Edward's voice came with a titanic migraine. In addition to the pain, he felt the embarrassment of someone catching him in a private moment. The second bell rang ten times as loud as the first, but Thomas couldn't get up. Edward was pushing his way in again, trying to take over.

I know what you're thinking. Why, oh, why didn't I just inject some paint thinner instead of taking that W?

So it really is the W that makes me like this. Was Edward confirming it, or was that just his own suspicion sneaking in through Edward's thoughts?

Annie would be coming into the atrium soon. She had second lunch. A few of Thomas's other friends were around, but they were too busy with the demonstration some celeb chef was putting on in the open kitchen. He struggled to stay in control. The truth was that he didn't have any. He was completely at Edward's mercy.

That's right, Tommy. Positive thing number five.

He had to keep fighting, because Edward *had* no mercy. When the late bell rang, Thomas looked up and saw Annie entering the atrium, holding a salad. Before he could duck out of sight, she noticed him and waved. Thomas nodded, then turned his head so she wouldn't see him cringe. Annie weaved through the demonstration crowd.

"Hey." She hugged him. He managed a friendly grunt. "Don't you have debate?"

"I do," said Thomas. He tried to leave before Edward could do anything, but his legs wouldn't obey. Instead, he found himself saying, **"Unless you want to go premarital in the bathroom stall."**

"What?" said Annie, blinking a few times too many.

"You know what I mean."

Stop! shouted Thomas in his mind.

Annie chuckled nervously. "Is everything OK?"

Thomas shouted as loud as he could, but the only sound in his head was Edward laughing.

"Yeah," said Thomas. "Bad joke."

He was surprised to gain a sliver of control over his body. He had to get away from Annie before Edward took over again just to toy with him.

"Sorry," said Thomas. "I really should get to debate. I was just being stupid."

"OK," said Annie. "See you later?"

"Absolutely," said Thomas. He grabbed his bag and rushed through the crowd. As he passed, the chef said, "And now, let's check on that roasting squash! Do you smell that sage? Ah, I just love that."

The crowd clapped at the squash. Thomas stumbled into the main building.

The halls were nearly empty. Everyone was either at lunch or in class. A maintenance guy was on a ladder, installing more security cameras. Thomas sidestepped the ladder and tried to avoid looking right into the camera. In the next hall, a janitor was taping a flyer to the door of the teachers' lounge. Thomas did a double take. It was an artist's rendering of a face he knew. The narrow eyes, the long black hair, even the semblance of a wicked grin—the sketch was Edward. The text on the flyer said: IF SEEN, REPORT IMMEDIATELY.

The janitor must have sensed Thomas's glare or heard him stop. He turned and said, "Anyone you know?"

Thomas snapped out of it. The janitor was looking at him expectantly.

Jesus Christ, thought Thomas.

Edward Hyde, actually. But I get that all the time.

"Hey, kid," said the janitor.

"What?" said Thomas, swallowing.

"You hear my question?"

"No," said Thomas. He turned and walked toward the debate class. Ever since the crimes, Marlowe had its private security on overtime. Of course, the parent pressure had gotten the police commissioner of New York personally involved in the cases. But with each day that passed, the school board was becoming antsy. Emergency PTA meetings had double their usual attendance. The school message boards were vibrating with alarmist frenzy.

And now they were placing cameras in every nook, and cops were pulling kids out of class for interviews.

It's becoming a witch hunt, thought Thomas.

Trust me. This is nothing like a witch hunt.

156

Thomas would have skipped debate, like every other extra-curricular activity he'd bailed on recently, but he just couldn't let Jenko Kolnikoff take over as captain for the tournament that weekend. For now he had the top spot on the team, and for Thomas, that was the only thing that gave him hope for the future. Everything else was fear of getting arrested, of losing himself to W, of being a prisoner to Edward.

Thomas stepped into the room in time to hear his newest rival, Jenko, an upstart freshman, say, "—not here, then I motion that he loses by forfeit."

"I'm here," said Thomas.

Jenko visibly deflated at his podium.

"Glad you made it, Thomas," said Mr. Finch.

The rest of the debate team sat at the desks facing the two podiums in the front of the room. Everyone had an accordion file full of briefs and a note-card holder with their arguments—both pro and con—for half a dozen issues facing America and the world. Thomas apologized to everyone and set his bag on the desk in front of his podium. He reached for the notes he'd prepared when Mr. Finch said, "You won't be needing those, Thomas. We're going to try a round on a subject none of you has prepared for—get some practice in case the judges throw in a wild card at the tournament."

"Oh," said Thomas, zipping the bag back up. "OK."

Thomas stepped behind his podium and tried to calm his breathing.

Nervous, sweet pea?

Shut up, Edward. Just shut up for twenty minutes.

Jenko was looking smug, nodding to the judges. The freshman

had achieved plenty just making the team, but he was one of those kids that was already thinking of public office at fifteen. No point trying to teach him that it's rude to cut in line.

Jenko, with his bleached-white hair, nonprescription glasses, and junior politico self-righteousness, was always turning reasoned debate rounds into demagogue training camp. Mr. Finch cleared his throat. The room fell silent. Mr. Finch loved the pregnant pause. He stretched the silence as far as it would go, then said, "Gentlemen, your prompt . . ." He took a moment to have a drink from his 5K Fun Run water bottle. Jenko twirled his pen over his thumb with angry little swipes. Thomas closed his eyes and hoped nothing bad would happen till he got home. Mr. Finch swallowed with a loud exhale and said, "Your prompt, gentlemen, is this: In light of recent events at Marlowe, administrators and parents have called in the NYPD to patrol our school, install surveillance equipment, and accost our students during the school day. This is above and beyond the private security team already in place."

Another pause. Thomas glanced over at his opponent. Jenko was furiously taking notes, as though this were new information. When he saw Thomas watching him, Jenko performed a double reverse spin of his pen, like a gunslinger twirling a pistol. Thomas rolled his eyes.

How about we rough him up just a little? Look at those beady little eyes.

Mr. Finch moved on. "The point we are arguing is this: Though some claim that escalation in security is doing more harm than good, the measures taken are necessary. Now, Mr. Jenko Kolnikoff, you will debate for this argument, while, Mr. Goodman-Brown, you will take the counter position. Pro goes first."

The stopwatch barely clicked before Jenko started at top speed. "The fact at hand is that we have a monster on the loose here in Marlowe, ladies and gentlemen. It followed Roger to a club, which implies stalking, then it brutally attacked. Now it's kidnapped a girl, who could have been any of you — and who knows what it's doing to her. . . ."

I know . . . I know exactly . . .

Something jumped in Thomas's chest. "Th — that's conjecture," he muttered.

"Now, now, Thomas," said Finch. "No interruptions."

Jenko went on: "I submit that the safety of the school is much more important than temporary freedoms or privacy."

Tell 'em it won't help. I like the attention. I like the pansy cops.

Thomas took a deep breath, then another. Mr. Finch eyed him and stopped the clock. "Mr. Goodman-Brown, are you all right?"

"Yes," whispered Thomas, then he cleared his throat and added, "a school has no right to suspend the personal freedoms of its students . . . to dig around in their lockers or read their journals, which is a violation of their private thoughts."

"Yes, thank you, Mr. Goodman-Brown," said Mr. Finch, looking perplexed. "But it isn't your turn."

"Sorry," said Thomas, feeling the beads of sweat dripping down onto his podium.

Are you feeling violated, Tommy? Do you need more privacy? Are you trapped, like a sad little housewife?

"Stop it!" Thomas said out loud. The room went silent. He could feel his body heating up. He took another deep breath to calm down. He knew Edward was waiting for him to lose control. Even worse. Thomas knew Edward didn't *need* to wait.

"I'm sorry," Thomas said again. "Let's go on. Really, I'm good."

Mr. Finch nodded and clicked the stopwatch.

Jenko continued. "If we don't increase security, search every locker, heighten our awareness of suspicious activity, how many others will be assaulted by this criminal?"

I like the way the kid thinks.

"That's not how the law works." A sweaty, red-faced Thomas jumped in, no longer caring about the stopwatch. "Those officers are part of a system. You can't just impose martial law in a school, doofus. And who're you to say that it's worse to be assaulted than to have zero freedom? **This isn't the motherland, Comrade.**"

Oh, God, did Edward just speak?

Someone in the back coughed the words "KGB fail."

"That wasn't my point at all!" said Jenko.

Thomas would have enjoyed watching Jenko squirm if he weren't struggling with every fiber of his being to hold Edward back. He gripped the sides of the podium so tightly that the particleboard began to squeak. Before Jenko could explain, he was interrupted by a voice much huskier than Thomas's. **"We know what your point was."**

Everyone looked at Thomas, or rather, at a version of him they hadn't ever seen before. Thankfully, the majority of the physical transformation hadn't happened yet. But the nice guy they all knew had a vicious grin as he said, **"Your point was that if we don't start burning suspects as witches, the world's gonna end."**

"I didn't say that," said Jenko.

Thomas slammed his palm on the podium, "***Buzz*, your turn's over, sweetheart. Let me tell you what they used to do in witch hunts. They'd strip you naked, and it didn't matter that you full well *admitted* to killing that whole village—they'd *still* interrogate you. And when the fat inquisitor leaned in too far—*snap!*"**

Edward chomped his teeth. A girl in the front row flinched. Thomas was helpless, watching the situation without any control over his actions.

"How do you like that for fearmongering, Jenko? We can all sit around telling torture stories from the old days, wear bow ties to a high-school debate class, and put on smug airs without offering a shred of evidence aside from the airtight proof that you're a wannabe political dickhea—"

"Mr. Goodman-Brown!" said Mr. Finch.

"I'm not Goodman-Brown!" shouted Edward, knocking over the podium. The clatter made the girl in the front yelp. Jenko was red in the face. His eyes betrayed his mix of anger, embarrassment, and the attempt to find a spin on the situation that meant victory. The rest of the class watched as the captain of their team, Thomas Goodman-Brown, grabbed his head and swayed back and forth. His legs looked like they would buckle any second. Was he coming down with something? Was he coming down *off* of something? He took a stumbling step toward Mr. Finch's desk and put a hand down to steady himself. His chest heaved as if he'd just run five miles.

"Thomas? Are you all right?" said Mr. Finch.

The room waited in silence. No answer.

"I vote we call the officer in the hall," said Jenko. "He's acting suspicious."

"Be quiet, Jenko," said Mr. Finch.

The first thing Thomas gained control over was his eyes. He started to blink, then focused on the calendar on Mr. Finch's desk to get his bearings. It was as if all his limbs had fallen asleep and now they were tingling all at once. Thomas groaned through the painful sensation. When he looked up, the whole class was staring at him.

"Uh. Sorry, everyone. I'm not feeling well."

He had to get home as fast as possible. He had just wanted this one thing to go well. But he should have known better.

"It's OK, Thomas. Why don't we pick this up later," said Mr. Finch.

Thomas reached for his bag. He leaned over to the girl in the front row and said, "Sorry for scaring you like that, Margie."

Thomas exhaled. No chance of going to the tournament now. Mr. Finch said, "You boys could use some research time. I'm sure Margaret can handle the tournament."

Thomas cringed as he slung his backpack on and walked to the door.

"Get well soon, Mr. Goodman-Brown," said Mr. Finch. Thomas nodded and trudged out into the hall. He glanced back over his shoulder as he left and saw Margaret gathering up her papers. Her hands were visibly shaking.

Positive thing number six: I think Margie likes me.

~~~~

That was bad. Bad. Thomas paced back and forth in his bedroom, trying to decide what kind of damage control he could possibly pull off now. Edward had put Thomas's entire life at risk during that disastrous debate class. Never before had he been so out of control so publicly. It was obvious now that Edward *wanted* to get caught. He wanted Thomas to be at his mercy, probably in a jail cell or a juvenile facility somewhere. What was Thomas supposed to do? And with the police interviewing everyone for their witch hunt, it wouldn't take long before they zeroed in on him — especially after they talked to Jenko. The commissioner already suspected him, and there was more than one career to be made on this investigation.

One thing that made Thomas feel better, though, was that for a second at the end of that debate class, he had gained control over Edward. He could feel it. He had breathed deep and focused his eyes on one object and had pulled himself out of the abyss. But somehow it didn't feel like enough.

It'll never be enough, Tommy.

That's it. No more waiting. Edward was getting stronger, and the only lead he had was the Fausts' old apartment. Thomas had to go back there and talk to whoever was living in that filthy ruin.

—⟳⟳—

Back on the dark street below the apartment, he watched their window, rotten tattered curtains blowing despite a lack of breeze, and thought of that last night with Belle. He shuddered at the memory of her face appearing behind the glass for only a second before she disappeared and he never saw her again. For so many nights after that, he had nightmares. She had become a monster.

He noticed a stream of insects flying out of a crack in the window.

I should just do this fast. No more waiting.

He crept into the abandoned lobby, then up the creaking stairs. Strangely, Edward had been quiet during the entire ride to the apartment. Maybe he was nervous. Maybe this was his true home and he wanted to see it again.

When he arrived at the dilapidated wooden door, he knocked twice. "Hello?" he called, trying to sound brave. "It's Thomas. Look, you can put down your weapons. I come in peace."

There was a shuffling inside. A whisper. But no one came to the door.

He knocked again.

He thought he heard voices inside, half sentences, like when you're trying to tune a radio and can catch only bits of words between static. ". . . can't . . . no door . . ."

Finally, Thomas took a deep breath and went for the door. It opened easily, but he took his time, making sure to look around before stepping inside. "I'm coming in," he shouted into the apartment.

When the door was ajar and he was inside, the first thing he noticed was the smell, the rancid odor of death. The floor was covered in dead bugs, old candle wax, balls of hair. "Oh, God," he muttered.

Then he looked up and saw two figures huddled in a corner.

One of them got up, picked up a small lamp beside him, and began to approach. For most of the way, his face was in shadow.

"What are *you* doing here?" said Valentin when he had reached Thomas.

Thomas was too shocked to respond. The sarcastic, confident

boy from last year, the kid who had swooped in and charmed everyone in school, was now an emaciated, sallow-cheeked creature with dirty hair and dead eyes.

Thomas looked away, pretending to survey his surroundings. It was a hellhole. Nothing like the pristine magazine-cover apartment he had visited last year. The floor plan didn't even seem to fit. How could this be? The apartment was round, with hallways branching out from a central room like spider legs. In the middle of the room was a huge dining table, with two legs broken, so that it slumped on one leg, the surface of it angled toward the floor like a playground slide. Holes peppered the walls, and when he looked closely, Thomas could see grotesque mounds of burned candle wax stuck like giant wads of bubblegum to every surface.

"I . . ." He didn't know how to answer Valentin. "Why aren't you in Geneva?"

Valentin laughed. In the distance, so did the owner of the second voice. Victoria scuttled toward them. Her movements were quick and careful, like a rodent who had been caught in too many traps. When he saw her, Thomas gasped. She was wearing the tattered remains of the exact dress she had worn to the Wirth Christmas party — on the very first night the Fausts were introduced in New York City.

She was squinting at him, as if trying to read his mind. Instinctively he stepped back. She scoffed. "Don't worry," she said. "I can't cheat anymore."

Thomas didn't know how to respond. He just said, "Huh?" and hoped his breathing wasn't audible.

"Read your mind," she said. "I can't do it anymore. FYI."

"I'm leaving," said Thomas, suddenly desperate for fresh air, to be away from this wretched place and from this horrible girl who had caused him so much grief last year.

Is Tommy scared? What's the matter? You don't like our house?

"Don't go," Valentin said. He sounded sad, even a little pleading. "Maybe hang out for a little while?" Thomas turned and looked him in the face. They had never been friends, but Thomas had seen a lot of Valentin last year, and seeing him without his signature bravado and confidence made Thomas feel sorry for the guy. He was twitching.

"Why aren't you in Geneva?" he asked again.

"Geneva?" said Victoria. "We never left this apartment."

Thomas looked around again, at the grimy walls, the branching hallways, the broken table, and the hellish light emanating from the blobs of wax. "This can't be the same apartment."

Victoria laughed. "Why not? Because pretty things are pretty forever?"

I like her. You know what, Tommy? I think we should stay.

Thomas tried not to shake. "Where's Belle? And Christian and Bicé?"

"Long gone," said Valentin. "The three of them ran off and left us here. You'll never find 'em. Wish I'd gone, too. . . ."

"So why don't you leave?" said Thomas. It was hard not moving toward the door every few seconds. He had this strange feeling that the exit might suddenly disappear.

Valentin gave a mournful, sardonic laugh. "You can't just walk out of prison. She's holding us here. . . ."

"But the door opened so easily —" said Thomas.

Valentin looked around with hungry eyes. What he said next

made Thomas want to turn and run and never come back. Valentin looked at the air just behind Thomas and said, "What door?" His expression was innocent and hopeful.

Nice one, Mom.

Now Thomas had to sit down. He dropped to the filthy floor. He rubbed his aching forehead with both palms. "Tell me about her," he said. He knew he didn't have to explain any more. Everyone in town knew that his father had recently married the governess. Victoria and Valentin must realize that Thomas, too, was in her clutches now.

"She's no governess," said Valentin. He had a faraway look in his eyes. The Valentin that Thomas knew was no longer there. He was a dead thing. A half zombie.

"No!" said Victoria. Thomas saw her scoop up a few dead bugs from the floor and whisper to them as if they, too, had a say in this decision. "Don't tell him anything!"

"Shut up," said Valentin. "Thomas, just stay away from Vileroy. She can do a lot of . . . bad things . . . very bad things to you."

"She's some kind of witch, isn't she?" said Thomas. "Black magic and all that. . . ."

Valentin shook his head. He stepped closer until his face was just a few inches from Thomas's ear. Then he whispered, "Not a witch. . . . She's a demon."

The chill that passed through Thomas's body might very well have frozen his organs and all the blood in his veins. How could that be true? It must be a game, or a dream, or hallucination. But, then again, how had the apartment changed so much? How had Victoria read his mind at last year's debate competition? How had the five Faust children accomplished so many extraordinary things in the short months that they'd been at Marlowe? He remembered now that Bicé spoke dozens of languages—a thing that had seemed only slightly odd back then because of all the time she spent studying—and that Christian had pummeled everyone in every sport he tried. That, too, hadn't seemed so strange at the time.

"Why . . . ?" He trailed off, not knowing how to finish.

"Because," said Valentin. "We sold our souls to her."

Now all Thomas could do was laugh. "You're kidding, right?" When Valentin didn't laugh, Thomas inched toward the door until he had one foot outside.

Valentin eyed him hungrily. "I can't see your foot anymore," he said, his voice now dreamy, as if in a trance. "Is that where the door is?"

Victoria, too, had now jumped up and was moving toward Thomas. "Yes!" she said. "That's the door! His foot is through the door."

Thomas was panting. "You . . . you really can't see this door?"

The two prisoners shook their heads. "Just walls," whispered Valentin.

Out of sheer pity, Thomas put his foot back in the room. "Will you guys help me figure something out?" he asked. "I think she's drugging me. I can't remember things anymore . . . and that night, when I came to dinner . . ."

Valentin didn't take his eyes off the spot. "She made you forget. She has potions."

"What kind of potions?" Thomas asked.

Victoria shrugged. "Ones that change your face and body, like the one Belle used. Ones that make you young, like the one Bicé used. Val and I never took any of her serums. You'd have to ask Belle and Bicé . . . but, like Val said, you'll never find them."

Already Thomas knew that he had to find them. There were so many questions unanswered. He knew now that what happened at the dance — that horrible moment when his beautiful girlfriend had become a monster — was a result of Vileroy's magic. He knew also that at various instances in the last year (who knows how many times), his own body had been infected with her serums and potions. He felt violated, though he realized the irony of it. He had put plenty of dangerous substances in his own body. Even now he held on to his new treasure, the bottle of W, like a security blanket.

Still, he was determined to find some answers.

He promised himself that he would find Belle and Bicé.

"I gotta go," said Thomas. "I'm sorry." He tried not to look at their desperate faces as he rushed toward the exit. But before he could leave, Thomas remembered something. "What about her son?" Thomas asked.

Victoria laughed.

Valentin's eyes widened at the horrible possibility — a reaction that made Thomas a hundred times more curious. "No way," said Valentin. "I'm her favorite. If she had a son, I'd know about it."

They all say that.

THE OTHERS

"How did the Egyptian girl lose her immortality?"

"Why are you so obsessed with these old stories, my friend? You've asked so often I think maybe this is the only reason you come to see me."

"I'm sorry. But I have to know, and you're the only bookseller who's read it all. Just tell me how to —"

"How to what, Bicé? These are just old legends. They mean nothing. But every time you come to my library, you are interested in only this one old myth."

"I'm curious. What do the legends say about how to kill a demon like her? I mean kill her for good."

"Oh, there are so many theories. Some said a simple crucifix to the eye would do it, but that only left her scarred. Some call on God and the angels. Others say it is a matter of human will. According to legend, she's hidden her life source in serums and potions over the millennia, but the last of it is now tied to her son."

"So what's the answer?"

"Nothing. She has found a host for her son's soul. He is weak, confused. Soon Hyde will return, and so will the demon Vileroy."

For days after the visit, Thomas was frantic. Should he call the police? Would they believe him? Clearly Vileroy was holding Valentin and Victoria by using some kind of magic. What could the police do against a demon? *I have to get out of town.*

But where? Thomas considered his options. He could visit his great-aunt in Berlin, or, better yet, his cousin who was a lawyer at the international criminal court in The Hague, or just go to some beach for a mini-holiday.

The thought resurfaced that the only way to be free from Edward and Edward's crimes was to find Belle and her twin sister, Bicé.

Now he was sure that all of these magic dusts had to be linked:

Bonedust and Bicé's potion both brought youth.

W and Belle's potion both altered physical appearance.

W and bonedust both healed wounds.

That made a full circle. All of these formulas must have the same source, or at least similar ones. According to John Darling, bonedust belonged to the missing school nurse, which was a dead end. He was left with Belle and Bicé. The thought of those happy months dating the beautiful Belle Faust sent a shiver of sadness through his body. He shook it off, summoning all his courage. He would have to find the missing Faust twins, wherever they were hiding.

He jumped up from his bed and plopped down at his desk, his foot tapping the floor as he waited the four seconds for his computer to turn on. He opened an Internet browser, but when he put his fingers on the keys, he realized he had no idea what to type. How do you search for three missing kids who may not want to be found? He searched some local missing children agencies but realized that no one would be looking for the Fausts. Their governess was the only person they had. His mind began to wander to Belle's room and all the beauty contest photos and clippings, and his fingers typed the words *beauty contest winner* before he snapped back to attention and chuckled at the stupidity of such a search.

Belle is ugly now.

What trace of herself would a girl that used to be beautiful leave on the Internet? How would you catch her scent? A good investigative lawyer would know exactly what to look for. A girl obsessed with beauty. A horrible face. Probably no money or resources. Probably living in a sleepy little town with low prices — somewhere no one from New York City would go. He began searching beauty forums where desperate women share low-cost tips. There were so many anonymous girls there, with names and concerns like hers. Any of them could have been Belle.

BelleF303: *I feel so ugly.*

Bellissima22549: *How do I make my nose look smaller?*

LadyBella.xxx: *Any tips on covering blemishes on a budget?*

BBNewJersey5: *Can you get crow's-feet at 17?*

IsabelleW623: *Who will love me now?*

It was exhausting reading their posts.

"Searching for beauty tips?"

Thomas jumped up and clasped his chest. He turned to face his best friend, Connor. "How did you get in?"

Connor shrugged. "I rang the bell. And then I knocked on your door. Why so distracted?" He peeked over Thomas's shoulder at the screen again.

Thomas sighed. No point in hiding *everything*. "I'm looking for Belle."

Connor's jaw dropped open. "Why? . . . And how? . . . And, also, *WHY*?"

"Never mind," said Thomas, turning back to his chair and the computer screen. "Look, I'll call you later."

"Hey, now," said Connor. "Look, if you need closure, I get it. Let me help. Did you try Geneva?"

Thomas shrugged. Connor leaned over Thomas's shoulder and stared at the chat-room conversation for a few seconds.

"Maybe it'd be better to search for Christian instead," he said finally. Thomas could hear in his put-on casual tone that he hated mentioning his old athletic rival. Connor continued, "He was always in the school paper for wins or records. Remember when he broke the record for longest drive? He ended up in city papers, too."

Of course. Christian's golf drive was so long he could have played in the Masters. Thomas remembered the fun they used to have, playing golf and making fun of stupid things. He held his breath as he typed, *Newcomer high-school champ breaks record.* A thousand hits. He scrolled through them one by one—each of them in a different state, different city—looking for someone with a cluster of wins in several different sports. Some stories had pictures and he could eliminate them quickly. Others had names that Connor entered into Facebook on his phone to make sure they weren't Christian.

"You know what?" said Connor, an hour and two sandwich

breaks later. He was leaning back on an ergonomic desk chair in the corner of Thomas's room, tossing and catching a tennis ball. "Christian *hated* sports."

Thomas turned in his chair. "I know, but he'd still play, right?"

Connor shrugged. "Maybe not. He's free to do whatever he wants, right?"

Thomas had never considered this — maybe because at Marlowe no kids got to choose what talents they *didn't* pursue. There were too many parents and counselors and teachers pushing them forward. Was it like that in the rest of the country? Probably not.

Last year Connor had almost drowned in a swim meet, and Christian hung his head and said he wished that they would just eliminate the sports program. He used to spend all his free time writing poems.

Connor jumped up from his chair and watched as Thomas typed, *Newcomer wins high-school poetry prize.* He scrolled past an article about a Chinese girl in Raleigh who taught herself English, past a thirteen-year-old boy from San Francisco and an angry girl with long hair looking disdainfully at her medal. Again, he focused on the ones in which one kid had won lots of different contests in one town.

Then, a photo from the *Sandy Cove Times* caught his eye. A boy with long reddish hair hanging over his eyes, just barely touching his gaunt cheeks, looking away from the camera as the school principal gave him a trophy. He seemed desperate to get off the stage. From the surroundings in the photo and the principal's shabby suit, he could tell that this was a small, overlooked town bordered by prettier cities. Every state has one — a Podunk place everyone else can look down on and feel lucky they don't live in. The picture was from a second-rate high school in a drive-through town on the way to somewhere better. He read the article out loud. The town was in Maine somewhere, and the boy was named Jamie West. Could this Jamie kid really be Christian Faust, his old friend, the Marlowe superstar? "Is it him?" he whispered, chills running down his back as he waited for Connor to respond. Connor only stared and shrugged.

There was no way to be sure. Jamie was so thin, the lines of his chin and jaw sunken and bony. He definitely didn't have Christian's Super Bowl build. In fact, he was swimming in his jeans and red button-up flannel shirt.

But that was definitely Christian's red hair.

"What about that one?" said Connor, pointing to another article in the Google search. "Try it." It was a local poetry and prose contest in south Texas, in a town called Midfield, and the big winner of the day was a boy named Christian Ford. Strangely enough, the boy refused to have his picture taken because of some crazy belief that the photos would suck out his soul and he would no longer be able to write.

Connor burst out laughing. "Are you freaking kidding me?" he said. "That's him. It *has* to be him!"

"No way," said Thomas. "That kind of fauxhemian creative crap doesn't sound like Christian at all."

"The name sure does," said Connor.

Thomas nodded. *Didn't Valentin and Victoria say that they had sold their souls to Vileroy?* Besides, if the Fausts were hiding from their evil governess, wouldn't Christian need *some* excuse to avoid being photographed? He almost wished he could tell Connor these last details.

As Thomas's thoughts drifted between Christian Ford and Jamie West, he thought of Belle again. Beautiful Belle weeping somewhere, hiding her face from the world, pouring her sorrow into some anonymous beauty chat room. Was she in Sandy Cove, Maine, or Midfield, Texas? "Hey, I have another idea," said Thomas. Hands shaking, he opened a news search engine and typed in, *Girl without face*.

"Crap! Look here." Connor pointed to the fourth hit. "That's just creepy."

Girl in Burka Refuses to Relent: Two months and still without face.

The story was about a brother and sister who had moved into a sleepy town and enrolled at the local high school. The girl wore a burka to orientation and again on the first day of school. When her teachers complained that they couldn't teach a girl whose face they had never seen, a small controversy arose. During the first month of school, the debate was quashed by many fervent references to freedom of religion and expression. But then someone found out that the girl's family wasn't Muslim at all. Strangely, the article said, the girl's brother was an agnostic of Scottish descent, and her single mother was just an old coot with a sweet smile and an optimistically oblivious attitude to the hereafter. Still, most school officials sided with the girl, claiming she could have her own personal beliefs. But then sparks flew once more, when they put the girl in an all-girl classroom and she still refused to take off the burka.

Thomas scanned the page for a photo. There was nothing helpful—just a snapshot of a figure with black coverings draping all

176

around her as she glided through a hallway of lockers, a dozen eyes on her as she went.

The article was from a town called Sandy Cove, Maine.

The girl's name was Isabelle West.

As his father's private jet sped down the runway and tilted upward, Thomas began to relax. He sipped sodas with Connor, crunched on some crushed ice, and thought about what he would say to Jamie and Isabelle — aka Christian and Belle. His foot continued to tap on the carpeted floor, half from nerves and half from the excitement of having cracked such a gargantuan mystery.

"You know," said Connor, "I've never seen a guy go to so much trouble just to get closure. Are you sure you're telling me everything?"

"I never tell you everything," said Thomas.

"Any more pita chips over there?"

Thomas tossed him a fresh bag from a minibar beside his chair. He was jittery with excitement. He had spent the better part of a day glued to his computer, reading article after article, and he had finally pieced everything together. When he asked his father if he could use the plane, his dad laughed and said, "No way," until he heard Thomas was going on a day trip with Connor. "Really?" he said. "You're hanging out with Connor again? Good, good. Yeah, have fun."

Then Thomas had spent another two hours researching and prepping what he would say to his old friends when he found them. It was hard work, but completely worth it. He promised himself that

he would do this again, maybe in a few years, when he was intern-
ing at a human-rights project, or later, as a junior lawyer in a firm
dedicated to pro-bono humanitarian cases. He would pay his dues
and crack tough cases, just as he had today. He would be exhausted
and hungry and it would feel so good.

A few minutes after leaving his pilot in a nearby private landing
strip, Thomas discovered that as small as Sandy Cove may be, without an address he was as lost as he would be in New York. He and
Connor spent half an hour asking around in the town center, which
consisted of a couple of stores, a church, a town hall, and a single
traffic light. There were at least three cafés, each with a homemade
wooden sign, in a town that probably had no more than a few hundred residents. Maggie's Café. Sylvia's Bakery and Tea Shop. Marie's
Old-Time Coffee. *They must really love coffee.* It was the owner of
Marie's who pointed them down a dusty road that seemed to lead
right out of the country.

"Can you hang around here till I get back?" said Thomas when
his friend started to follow him down the road.

"No way!" Connor protested. "I came all this way."

"I know," said Thomas, thinking of his many unspeakable
secrets — and everything the Fausts would reveal. "But I have to do
this alone, OK?"

The look on Connor's face made Thomas feel like the worst
friend ever, but he was relieved when Connor didn't object. He said,
"Fine, but you owe me one," and turned back into the café, muttering glumly about how he should have stayed home.

"I owe you about a hundred," Thomas called after him.

Twenty minutes later, Thomas was standing in front of a

cottagelike house situated by itself at the end of a small road, with thick curtains covering the windows and a lawn with a hodgepodge of mismatched flowers, as if they had been planted by a blind person. The mailbox said BEATRIX WEST.

He knocked twice. When the door finally opened, he found himself staring at a strange old woman with a familiar face. He held out his hand and said, "Hello, Miss . . . Beatrix . . . um . . . pleasure to meet you."

She looked at him for a full minute, her lips quivering, before she spoke. "Thomas Goodman-Brown," she said. "Why did you come?" She took his hand into her warm, veiny grasp and held it there — the gesture of someone used to playing the grandmother.

"I'm sorry?" he said, pulling back. "How do you — I mean — I'm looking for Jamie and Isabelle West."

The old woman began mumbling something in another language. Then she snickered to herself, shook her head, and said, "It's me, Bicé. Do you remember me? From our days in school?" She spoke as if it had been a hundred years ago that they had been classmates.

For a moment, Thomas couldn't breathe. He looked deep into her face, all the parts of it that had looked familiar to him before. The nose, the almond-shaped eyes, the pretty half smile, still kind of young and girlish. She was exactly like Bicé Faust, the soft-spoken outcast who used to sit for hours in the library, used to ride back and forth aimlessly on the subway, and used to watch her brothers and sisters compete against Thomas and his friends in contests and tournaments and meets.

He didn't know what to say. He mumbled, "Victoria said you were . . . older."

She laughed. "Now, that is a long, long story. Do you want to come inside?"

He didn't, but he nodded and entered the house. Inside was dim, but he could smell lavender, and something baking. The house was decorated with old furniture, probably from secondhand stores, mismatched, some of it frayed, but overall cozy and warm, arranged around the room by someone with an eye for beautiful things. There was a small lamp covered in a pink lamp shade on a corner table. It cast a rosy light into the room. Bicé offered him a plate of random cookies, homemade, but all different kinds. He took one and said, "I came because I need your help."

She nodded, as if she knew, then she plopped down onto an armchair and motioned for him to sit. "I'll do everything I can, Thomas." She waited and Thomas tried to find a good starting point. When he didn't start right away, she added, "Is *she* still there, hanging around your circle?"

Thomas nodded. "She married my father."

He saw Bicé bite her lip, then nod.

"Look, I know when the three of you lived with her, she gave you potions and things. I think she's poisoning me. Do you remember that night? At your house?"

Thomas could see Bicé's face closing up, as if some deep sadness were taking over. "I'm sorry about that, Thomas. That was the night I found out what she really was. I didn't mean for bad things to happen to you."

Thomas smiled. "How do I know if she's drugging me? Bad things are happening—" Thomas stopped. Should he tell Bicé about all the partying and drugs and everything he had done since Belle

180

left? She looked so much like a mother, or grandmother, that his natural instinct was to keep his secrets. But he reminded himself that Bicé was just an unlucky girl his own age.

Just then, there was a noise and the door creaked open. In the doorway stood the gaunt redheaded boy from the award ceremony photo. His greasy hair came down over his eyes and he was about fifty pounds thinner, but that was definitely Christian Faust staring openmouthed at Thomas from the doorway. Thomas got up from his chair. "Christian," he said, and held out his hand. "Good to see you again, buddy."

Christian didn't move.

He looked off in the direction of the only small hallway in the house. For an awkward moment, everyone stood silently, biting nails and fidgeting. Then Christian said, "Why are you here?"

"I just . . . It's Vileroy," said Thomas. "Is Belle here?"

Christian didn't answer. He just stood there squinting, then moved to the small couch and sat at the edge, pushing a chunk of hair behind his ear. He stared at the plate of cookies but didn't take one, just looked up at Thomas and waited with empty eyes. Thomas sat down, too, and began to explain about the bottle of W and about Nikki, about the flashes of black and changing into someone else. He told them about how each pill was a different component of his alter ego and that he felt a different one of Edward's emotions each time. He talked about the gradual change into Edward, first in his thoughts and then his body. He told them about the recent crimes at Marlowe, about Roger and Marla and the missing school nurse. It seemed like he spoke for an entire hour. Bicé and Christian never said a word, only looked at each other once in a while, as if communicating on some other level. They might have had a whole conversation that Thomas couldn't hear. Those two always did seem closer than any of the other Faust kids.

Finally, when Thomas was finished, Christian spoke: "Can I see this W?"

Thomas hesitated. Then he reached into his pocket, took out the bottle, and set it carefully on the coffee table next to the cookies. Christian took it, popped it open, and unceremoniously emptied the contents onto the table. Thomas gasped but didn't object.

Bicé picked up one of the pills, held it up to the light, and turned it over, bringing it closer to her foggy, sunken eyes. "Yes," she said. "Yes . . . this is Nicola's work." She looked up at Thomas. "I wouldn't see this Nikki person again."

"How can you be sure?" said Thomas.

"I've roamed her house for a hundred years, Thomas," she said. "I know the smell of this pill. It has the same sludge smell from the potion she used to give me." She pulled away from the tablet as if she were tempted to swallow it right there. Thomas wondered just how much of an addict Bicé had been. A hundred years? Who would waste their whole life that way? And how was she still alive? Thomas couldn't even tell how old she looked. She looked different in every light. Sometimes no more than fifty, sometimes so old he didn't dare dream up a number.

He tried to make a joke. "So if I take all of it, I won't just change into Edward but I'll live forever, too? Great."

No one laughed. Bicé shook her head and said, "*Hyde* will live forever. Not you. *You* will probably die."

It wasn't the words but something in her tone, the whispered warning, that made Thomas shiver. "He calls himself that sometimes. Hyde. How did *you* know?"

The old woman sighed. She looked into Thomas's face and said, "Last year, I tried to kill her. I tried to learn the ancient language that no one can learn in one lifetime, because you have to know all languages. But it only weakened her. It didn't kill her because she was hiding a secondary source to her immortality. I read news reports and talked to many people and pieced together that she was posing as the school nurse to protect the bones of her ancestors, this so-called *bonedust*. I just didn't know she had another—"

"Hold on a sec," Thomas interrupted. "She was posing as what, now?

Bicé shrugged. Thomas sighed. "Sorry. Go on," he said.

"I didn't know she had another backup. You see, she let her supply of immortality become depleted. She was so eager to advance herself with its power, she spread it too thin. She hid bits of it in beauty potions and age-masking serums, small things to help her trap people like us. Then, in her eagerness to protect it, she did the last desperate thing a demon can do. She had a son. Your *Hyde*. She killed him and mixed his body with a large portion of the bone-dust. I read about this ancient kind of magic. It's bad. Very bad. It means that she resigned herself to dying along with the pills, knowing that the tablets with Edward's body and soul were the last thing that could carry on her line. She has carried that bottle around with her for centuries as insurance. I saw it in her house once, hidden behind four doors. I reached out and almost touched it, and suddenly she was there, pushing me back into the real world. She has been searching for someone for years, someone with power, with resources, with just the right circumstances, waiting to create an immortal Edward and live on through his soulless demon children."

"So you're saying . . ." Thomas swallowed. This was too much to hear. How could he have taken those pills? The sight of them disgusted him now. He was the one responsible for his blackouts and for the bouts of change that overtook him. He had actually, physically, put Edward into his body.

From the corner of his eye, Thomas saw a black-shrouded figure appear, then disappear at the end of the hallway. Was it Belle lingering there, listening, keeping just out of sight? He felt sorry for her. She, too, had made an awful choice without knowing the consequences. He wished she would join them so he could tell her that he never cared about how she looked. But he knew Belle enough to know that she never would. She was content to stay in her corner, alone.

Bicé nodded. "You have a choice. You are already halfway there, if I'm counting these pills correctly. Edward is half inside you, half in that bottle. You could take them all and become Edward Hyde. Or you could abandon the pills and live in limbo."

Thomas felt the blood rush to his face. Panic began to take him over, that feeling of being trapped, like that awful night last year when Victoria meddled inside his mind at Vileroy's apartment. "Um . . . look, I was only kidding before about taking the rest of the pills. You said I'd die! Why on earth would I want to become Hyde? Why would I take the rest? Forget it. Toss them, for all I care!"

Christian snickered. "Nothing is that simple with her," he said, his voice raspier than before.

Bicé nodded. "It's true. It's not so simple. If you toss the pills, someone else can always find them. I have no idea how to destroy

184

them, so you can never be sure in whose hands they will end up. Vileroy could get them back. She would then have half of Hyde and could go on and on with her games, bring him back through some other weaker person. As for you, well, you would still have enough of him in you to torment you for life."

"And if I keep taking the rest?" said Thomas.

"It would be you against Hyde. . . . No more tablets. No more chances for him to come back. It would be riskier, tougher — life or death for you both. But at least the one who wins gets it all, a normal life instead of some pathetic half existence."

"Great," said Thomas, trying to steady his breathing.

"She's all about the ironic megachoices," muttered Christian. "I, for one, would go for the risky choice. Live free or die young, right?" He chuckled again. Thomas didn't remember Christian being so angsty. But then Christian flashed his old-boy smile and Thomas felt reassured. Maybe his friend was right. Thomas shouldn't go on like this. He should fight back.

"I thought that if I take the pills, Edward will take over," said Thomas. "That's what you said before."

"Yes," said Bicé. "That is how it's intended to work. It's how it works almost all the time, and so the old manuscripts and spells don't bother to mention the small, meaningless formalities. But the fact is, you can't take a person's soul without their permission. There are dormant powers inside everyone waiting to be called on. It may be nearly impossible to stop him, but Hyde *can't* take over unless you let him. He can't stay if you manage to toss him out." Thomas remembered that moment of overcoming Edward in debate class. It had been so hard to gain just a second, how could he ever do it for good?

You will never win. Never.

"But then . . . where would he go if the pills are gone?" he asked, ignoring Edward. He glanced down the hallway again, wondering if Belle would come back. But she was gone now. Maybe the shrouded figure he saw wasn't even her, just a shadow.

Bicé raised a gray-and-white eyebrow. She gave Thomas a big childlike smile, the way she used to do when they were the same age, and whispered, "Exactly. He will be imprisoned. No more Hyde. No more immortal Vileroy."

Nicola sat at her mirror and considered her surroundings. Something had changed. What was it? A mother always knows when her child is in danger. It is an instinct, deep inside. It comes even to the worst of mothers — the ones whose depths hold nothing but cobwebs and fire and malice. A child is your own legacy. Your own soul.

What was different now? Edward was safe. She knew this because she watched him from afar, when he revealed himself through Thomas and when he sat dormant in a glass bottle . . . waiting.

The room was half in shadow, half lit by three candles pooling wax on the late Mrs. Goodman-Brown's vanity table. Nicola touched her face. It was the face of the beautiful governess, not the nurse, but something was wrong. Was that a wrinkle? A new line? Or perhaps it wasn't new at all, but a very old line — one she had seen on the face of a hunchbacked nanny from long ago.

Things have changed.

Time is almost up.

15

MOTHER

Journal entry #32

Well, now the golden boy thinks he's gonna get rid of me. What a trip. He doesn't even know I'm writing this. He thinks he's sleeping. Stupid old girl in Podunkville . . . I wanted so much to get my hands around her withered old throat.

   Can't sleep.

   No! Let go, Mother! Let me go! I'll be good.

   What was I saying? No one gets rid of Edward Hyde. No reason to take Tommy boy seriously. Look at him and look at me. He doesn't stand a chance.

   Roger didn't stand a chance.

   And Marla. The screaming. You call that goth? I didn't even touch her. She was just afraid of the dark.

     ❖ ❖ ❖

As he rushed through the hallways of Marlowe, Thomas couldn't help but stop and look at Bicé's old locker. He had barely glanced at it the entire time she was here. And now it was being used by an exchange student from Karachi. He wondered if there were any remnants of Bicé left on the shelves, maybe a book or a photo tacked up to the door. Since returning from his trip to visit the "West" family, he had found himself thinking a lot about her, and now he wondered why he had spent most of last year completely ignoring the most fascinating and wonderfully bizarre person he had ever met. Maybe there were other fascinating and wonderfully bizarre people that he was ignoring now, just because they're too shy, or raise their hand too much in class, or are too science-y. Suddenly, he remembered that he owed John Darling some wall posts. He took out his phone and pulled up John's page. He tried to think of something to write on John's wall. He figured something vague and mildly conspiratorial would serve John's purposes.

Hey, buddy, I haven't forgotten our deal!

Just as he pressed ENTER, Thomas noticed his hands. They were dirty, as if he had been digging in mud. He felt a sharp ache in the back of his head. He looked at his phone, still on John's page. There were two messages on John's wall. Wait, had he just typed that second one?

You're next, nerdling.

Thomas dropped his phone. His hands were shaking, and his knees began to give out. The ache was getting worse. He had to do something, and he had to do it this second, before anyone read that post. He fumbled on the ground for his phone, even though his vision was beginning to blur and some passing freshman girls stopped to watch. And was that a police officer in the distance? Was he watching? He tried to calm his breathing, then picked up the phone and deleted the comment. He sent John a private message.

Sorry about that. Some jerk stole my phone.

Almost immediately, John wrote back. It was as if he had been waiting by his phone for messages.

No problem! But post on the wall, so everyone can see. This doesn't count.

Thomas rolled his eyes. He breathed in four or five times. Now he felt himself beginning to regain control, and he continued toward calculus. As he turned a corner, he wondered why he was even bothering to go. He was so far behind in that class that he wouldn't understand a thing anyway.

As he was reaching for the door, someone tapped him on the shoulder.

"Everything OK, son?" said the police officer he had seen in the distance. He was taller than Thomas and had a mustache, as if he thought he was in an '80s police drama.

I wonder if he's ever fired that gun.

Shut up. Shut up.

"Excuse me, son?" said the police officer, reaching for his belt.

Wait, did I say that out loud?

"I'm sorry, Officer," Thomas mumbled. "I wasn't talking to you. I was just . . . um . . . Anyway, yeah, I'm fine. Just going to class now."

He started to open the door again, but in a flash the officer's hand was back on his shoulder, gripping hard. He pulled Thomas toward him as if he wanted to smell his breath. "Have you been drinking?"

"No!" said Thomas, a little too eagerly.

"Then what were you doing back there? Fumbling around and talking to yourself like a loon? You better explain fast, son."

Thomas was about to dig around for an answer when he remembered something. Who the hell was this guy to tell him what to do? Wasn't he the one who wanted to be an ace lawyer someday? Nowhere in the many law books he had read in the past two years did it say that America was now a police state. Screw Jenko and the commissioner and their witch hunt.

"Excuse me, sir," he said in his most confident cross-examination tone, "but I'll thank you to remove your hand from my body."

The officer smiled, then chuckled and pulled his hand off Thomas's shoulder. "Are you stoned?" he asked.

"Am I under arrest?" said Thomas.

"You will be if I suspect you're high," he said.

Thomas ran his hand through his hair and mustered up all his courage. The guy couldn't touch him. This was a private school, and he had nothing to say to this loser. He looked the officer straight in the eyes. "Well, am I stoned or high? Which is it? Because they're not the same thing, Officer." He smiled big.

The officer narrowed his eyes. "Don't play cute with me, kid. I've been watching you. If you don't shape up and answer some questions, you're gonna be in a whole mess of trouble."

OK, maybe that was too much. Thomas wasn't even sure that last comment was his own. Sure, he was thinking it, but he didn't want to say it. The officer was reaching for his handcuffs now. *Oh, crap.*

Before the cop could touch him again, Thomas clutched his backpack and took off in a run down the hallway.

"Hey, stop right there!" the officer shouted behind him. But soon Thomas had turned three or four corners and disappeared toward the administrative offices. Maybe the principal would help. How could the police just swarm Marlowe like this, search lockers, interview students without their parents, and dig around for clues without permission from the kids or any real evidence of wrong-doing? The PTA must have been scared into agreeing to this. After all, both the Marla and the Roger incidents had happened outside of school. They had no reason to believe they could find evidence here. This was completely illegal, not to mention an insane abuse of authority. Yes, he would go to the principal and say just that, like a real lawyer. *This is an insane abuse of authority.*

In front of the office, he heard the officer's voice rushing in his direction. As his hand glanced over the door handle of the administrative office, Thomas began to lose confidence. Maybe this was the wrong move. What would happen to Thomas if the officer and Principal Stevenson trapped him in a room? They wouldn't just let him go. Would they let him call his dad? What if Edward chose that moment to come out?

Just as he was about to take off toward the courtyard, another option began to take shape. *Dr. Alma.* She had been so eager to help him, and even though he found her annoying and pushy, she was probably the only person who cared enough to check up on him each and every week. She was also legally obligated to keep her mouth shut, which was a major bonus at this point.

Outside Dr. Alma's office, a thought occurred to him: the worst thing that could happen wasn't jail. It was being unveiled as the other half of Edward, something freakish and supernatural. What would happen then? He thought of the Faust family, who had been driven away, and Valentin and Victoria, imprisoned in the penthouse from hell.

What other crimes has Edward committed?

Dr. Alma opened the door to her office with a nervous smile.

"Hello, Thomas," she said, pushing a pin back into her hair with both hands. She looked red in the face and her voice was hoarse, as if she had been in a screaming match. Thomas rushed inside and shut the door behind him.

"Dr. Alma, I need to —"

He stopped. In the far end of the office, behind Dr. Alma's desk, in a corner almost hidden by a long curtain, stood his stepmother, Nicola.

"What are *you* doing here?" Thomas spat. His heart began to pound faster and faster, and then, in a different voice, he heard himself say, **"Hello, Mother."**

His mouth tasted funny: dry and sour, as if he had drunk too much bad wine over many long, thirsty hours. Then, a second later, his mouth didn't taste like anything at all.

"Dr. Alma . . . I . . . don't want her here." He managed to toss the words out one by one, each with great effort, as if Edward were trying to stop him.

I want her here. She can help me kill you.

"It's only a parent-teacher conference," said Nicola innocently. "And I'm so glad you're here now, dear. Let's talk about your progress."

"No!" Thomas was struggling, clutching his head, fighting with Edward for control of his own body. He could feel the beads of sweat

192

dropping from his hair, his thoughts changing, the scents around him becoming just a little sharper, as if smelled through a different nose. How long had it been since he took W? How long would he have to put up with this?

"She's . . . she's the one . . ." he sputtered, spit flying from his mouth as he tried to force his tongue to make the syllables he, not Edward, wanted. "She made . . . W."

"Ah, yes," said Dr. Alma, her voice still a little nervous. She gave a small, inappropriate giggle and then stopped herself by clearing her throat. "The W . . . Have you followed my . . . um . . . advice? Did you take some more, or did you make the mistake of going cold turkey?"

Dr. Alma stood there, feet together, batting her eyelashes, sweating under Madame Vileroy's hard gaze, like the lowest thug in the presence of the godfather. He stared at her. She looked so much like Thomas's mother; he had always thought so. Maybe that was what made him talk during their sessions. He glanced down at her hand, nervously tapping her thigh, and noticed the ruby bracelet, just like the one his mother wore. Suddenly Thomas knew. All the details came together. Look at her, standing there, with her sandy hair and high cheekbones, trying to look like a mother, trying to look like *his* mother. Vying for his trust as only an untrustworthy person does. No, Dr. Alma wasn't on his side at all.

All those journal entries he'd written, all the personal information he had handed to her, and here she was, practically feeding him the W. How could he have missed it?

He wanted to bolt, but something kept him pinned to his spot. It felt very much like that night at her apartment, a connection that frightened him more than Edward's unending struggle to break out.

"My dad will find out," he whispered, hoping Vileroy could hear.

"Well," Vileroy said, waving away his comment as if it caused her no trouble at all, "I don't know what you're implying, dear. But having talked to your doctor, I can see well enough that whatever this drug is, it has had a permanent effect on you. I doubt very much that you can escape it, dear. Look at you. You're practically foaming at the mouth. Your face is white. Your hands are shaking. What a mess you are! And how sad to think that you did this to yourself."

She shook her head knowingly. The smug look on her face, and the way she made Dr. Alma cower, made Thomas want to reach out and strangle her. He took a step forward and then stopped himself.

Instead, he said, "I met someone you know."

Nicola's eyes narrowed. Thomas could see that she was curious as she tilted her head and tried to look nonchalant. But he knew that inside she was like a dog salivating for a slice of meat. She waited with total control.

"You can't make me take any more W," he said. "And you can't make me stop. You can't do anything, because I have the rest of it."

"Oh, darling," she said sweetly. "I don't care about what you do with those things. Your father and I only want you to get better." She shifted from her corner, inching closer to Dr. Alma's desk. The way she moved — so stealthily and noiselessly that the curtain didn't even ruffle — made Thomas want to step away.

"You think I'm stupid enough to toss it?" he said, summoning all courage. "So you can find it again?"

Madame Vileroy shrugged. Only her shoulders moved, nothing

else — not eyes or lips or head or a single strand of hair. Something in her left eye flashed — that creepy broken cross — and a moth fluttered around her hair.

Thomas finally wrestled back control over his feet. He grabbed the door and slammed it open, a little too hard. Then, just as he was about to run outside, he looked his stepmother in the eyes and said, "I'm going to kill Edward."

<hr/>

Nicola closed the door of the girls' bathroom. Thomas's words rang in her ears.

I'm going to kill Edward. I'm going to kill Edward.

Something must be done.

She took two deep breaths, then lifted her broken eye to the mirror outside the stalls. Her face looked tired, like so many of the weary mothers who think they are hiding the years beneath layers of makeup and chemical treatments. She had visited Dr. Alma because Thomas's progress was far too slow. Thomas had to be forced to take the W, all of it, very soon. If he didn't, Edward might die. But then Thomas had walked in and Dr. Alma had been exposed.

He must take those pills. But who would convince him? Not Dr. Alma. Not Nikki.

She glanced at her face again. She could still see a little of Nikki in certain lights.

She would have to put Thomas in a desperate position. A life-or-death moment. She moved slowly to the door, passing her fingers over the mirror. A moth followed a safe distance behind as she glided into the hallways of the Marlowe School.

16

DISTURBING BEHAVIOR

Journal entry #37

This journal is starting to feel like a legal brief or a state-ment of confession — I'm not sure which. I think I should keep recording the stuff I find, though, in case Edward wins. Maybe someone will find it and realize what happened.

The other day, I saw some files on Dr. Alma's desk with my name all over them. When she turned her back, I pulled on the corner of a piece of paper that looked like a news-paper clipping. I stuffed it in my pocket and read it in the bathroom. It was an article about a woman in Florida who left her kids in the parking lot of an airport. No one knows where she went. A baggage guy said he saw her with a blond lady. The last line of the article said she left a husband, the two kids, and a thriving psychology practice. The picture was of Dr. Alma.

After I win, I'm gonna burn this journal.

❖ ❖ ❖

Freaking hell-spawn demon witch-queen evil monster!

Thomas turned to run out of the office, screaming expletives in his mind — unsure whether the words were his or Edward's. And in those few seconds, he didn't care. He swung open the door and dashed past the secretary's desk into the waiting area. He remembered coming to this office last year — back when everything was simpler and he didn't come to have his head shrunk. He had sat in a chair reading college catalogs until the principal came out and handed him some award he couldn't even remember anymore. Now Thomas scrambled past the little glass table covered in catalogs, about to be framed for crimes he *only sort of* committed, or live forever imprisoned in his own mind, or maybe go brain-dead as soon as Edward took over completely.

Thomas cursed again as he slammed his knee into the corner of a chair. He ran out of the administrative office and into the hall.

Where am I going? I can't go anywhere.

His thoughts were cramming in so fast they were incomprehensible. Somewhere within them, he heard Edward.

You're done, Tommy. Don't make this ugly. You're done.

Thomas sprinted down the hall. He took a corner at full speed. Three cops, including Detective Mancuso and the guy with the mustache, were walking right toward him but hadn't seen him yet. They were looking into the atrium. Thomas skidded to a stop. His sneakers squealed as he wheeled around and turned back around the corner. He was sure the cops had caught a glimpse of him. Thomas ran back into the admin office. Behind the secretary's desk were three doors — the principal's office, the VP's, and Dr. Alma's. To his left, a short hall led to the temporary nurse's office — the real infirmary,

197

which used to be up in the attic, was now under repair because of some giant infestation earlier this year. After speaking with Bicé and John Darling, Thomas had some idea what the infestation had been — a room full of dead moths.

Thomas shuddered, thinking about Nicola posing as the plain-faced school nurse, pretending to take care of the students while trying to get close to his father. Thomas didn't have time to check any of the doors to see if Vileroy was still there. He glanced over his shoulder and saw the cops through the window. They rounded the corner and walked toward the admin office. Thomas ducked and ran toward the darkened nurse's office. Once inside, he scooted around the examination table, into a medicine closet. If he tucked his knees into his chest, he could just fit on the bottom shelf. He kept the door slightly ajar so he could get some air and so he could hear.

He was hyperventilating. Maybe that was it. He needed to control the intake. Thomas held his breath, then exhaled and made even more noise catching his breath again. *Calm down. Just calm down. Count to three. One. Two. Three.*

The door all the way out in the administrative office opened and a cop's voice drifted toward him: "I don't know. Wasn't like he sat for a portrait. All I saw was brown hair."

Thomas breathed a sigh of relief. They hadn't seen him. Not exactly. Detective Mancuso probably could have guessed, the way Thomas had been acting in front of him the last few days. Thomas stared at the door to the makeshift infirmary, waiting for a pair of shoes to block out the light coming from the hall. Nothing. He counted. *One. Two. Three.* Nothing.

You heard Mom. Game's over. You lost, Thomas.

No, thought Thomas. *You're lying.*

Thomas heard a grisly laugh. **Why would I lie? I don't just have you by the balls. I have you by the brain.**

'Cause if it were really over, you wouldn't care what I thought. You want me to give up.

The laughter stopped. Thomas braced himself, but Edward's voice was surprisingly calm. **Now, where was this clever Thomas when you were popping W and chasing club trash?**

Down the hall, Thomas heard Madame Vileroy's voice: "How can I help you, officers?" Her French lilt seemed doubly affected.

There's something holding you back, or else you'd kill me without any stupid ceremony.

Inside his crowded mind, Thomas heard only a conspicuous silence. The cops murmured something Thomas couldn't make out. His legs were starting to ache in the cramped space. It smelled like bandages and antiseptic. Vileroy's response was just loud enough for Thomas to hear — probably by design. "I'm here speaking with Dr. Alma. Have you met Marlowe's counselor? Yes. . . . Oh, no, not for any particular reason, no. I'm concerned for my stepson, Thomas Goodman-Brown, to be honest."

The cops said something else. Their tone had become higher pitched.

"Yes, that's him," said Vileroy. She was so good at sounding normal. She must have spent centuries perfecting the lie that she was human. She had an elegance that made people nervous. And when they're nervous, they don't question anything. They just want to stop being nervous. That's how the cops sounded, even though Thomas couldn't make out their words. They were infatuated and intimidated at the same time.

"His whereabouts?" said Vileroy. "Oh, I wouldn't know that. I was hoping that he would be here, seeing his counselor. I was hoping to consult the school nurse as well, but she has missed more than a few days of work. Our little Thomas might be in need of rehab."

Thomas could barely make out Detective Mancuso's words: "Check out the nurse's office."

A searing pain exploded behind Thomas's eyes, as if he'd been kicked in the back of the head with a steel-toed boot. It was Edward, thrashing around inside him. Thomas felt his esophagus closing from the pressure of something clamping around it. Then he heard Edward. *Let me explain something, little boy. I'm not your pet devil. I'm not your "mean side." I'm here to eat you — then to use those soft little fingers of yours to strangle the life out of Marla.*

With that, the grip on Thomas's throat clenched further. Thomas gagged for more air. His legs twitched, then began to visibly spasm. The cops were walking toward the infirmary. They'd soon hear any noise he made. Thomas felt the muscles in his face tighten over his jaw. He was changing into Edward. The voice of Detective Mancuso was close enough this time for Thomas to hear it perfectly. "Check if the nurse's got a calendar on her computer or an away message on her e-mails."

Thomas's entire body was vibrating with pain. His every instinct said to kick out of the medicine closet and give his body over to whatever Edward wanted. But somehow, the thought of giving up and dying in a closet after everything — after surviving his mom, falling for Belle only to watch Vileroy ruin her, and, now, seeing Vileroy set her sights on Thomas and his dad — after all that, it just seemed selfish. Thomas might be the only person to know Vileroy for what she was. If he didn't stop her, or at least fight her off, then there would be a dozen or more girls like Belle. She would trick more men like his dad. She'd steal more people like Dr. Alma for her servants. She'd cheat people out of their lives and lie to them until they gave her what was most valuable. And finally, whenever it was time to set things right, she would hide in the shadows and let people like Thomas take the punishment for what she and her son had done.

Someone had to save Marla — and pay them back for Roger.

Thomas found new strength in the idea and focused on pushing Edward back.

One. Two. Three.

I'll give you one thing, said Edward, his voice strained. ***You're not the weakling Mother said you are.***

Thomas heard the clatter of an officer's shoes on the marble floor outside the nurse's office. The thin strip of light turned into darkness. Thomas regained enough composure to stay silent just as they entered. As the door to the infirmary opened and spilled the light of the hallway into the room, the door to the medicine closet gently closed.

"Don't know what he expects to find," said the voice of one officer, "but for my sake, I hope that nurse is shacked up in Atlantic City right now with her boyfriend."

"Why is that, Tony?" said the other voice.

Thomas heard the familiar chime of a computer booting up.

"What do you mean, why? 'Cause if she ain't AWOL on some spontaneous booze weekend, then she's tied up in some psycho's basement. She's probably the third victim of the same crazy kid that attacked the other two. Do you know how much paperwork that is?"

Thomas caught his breath. This is exactly what Nicola must have wanted — to make them think that the nurse was Thomas's third victim, to make him culpable for even more hideous crimes. Several drawers ground open on their rollers, then closed again. A file cabinet squealed, got stuck, then lunged open.

Thomas wouldn't last much longer. He was losing grip once again, and by the sounds of it, the cops would find him any second.

I could kill them both.

"I don't see anything on her computer about a vacation, Tony."

"Great. Now we got another missing persons to write up, about a dozen acquaintances to interview, dust her apartment, make a timetable of last known whereabouts — just great."

"Let's just get outta here."

The computer clicked off. The file cabinet rattled shut.

"Check the closet before we go."

The clacking of shoes on marble. *One. Two. Three.*

Come on, let's kill them.

No! thought Thomas. The cop would open the door any second. It occurred to Thomas that Edward had asked his permission just then. And if he had asked permission, it meant he couldn't take control. At that moment, when Thomas was milliseconds away from being discovered, he formed a plan. Though he had never allowed himself to think deeply about it (Edward might be listening), the idea had begun to take shape the day Bicé told him that he had a choice to take the rest of the W. It was *his* choice, his fight to the death.

But no one could have foreseen what Thomas would do next. Not even Thomas.

The doorknob turned.

Thomas reached into his pocket, grabbed the bottle — all the W that was left — and swallowed all the pills at once. They jammed in his throat like a fistful of rocks, but he swallowed harder, forcing them down.

The officer opened the closet door. "What the —?"

A husky teenager with long dark hair lunged out of the medicine closet and grabbed the cop by the throat. Instead of reaching for his gun, the officer panicked and grabbed the stranger's hands. He tried to pull them off his throat, but the stranger was stronger.

"Put your hands up!" screamed the mustachioed cop from across the examination table, but no one was listening. He pulled his firearm and trained it on the struggling pair. He couldn't take the shot without risk to his partner.

"Outta the way, Jimmy. Get outta the way!" He reached up to his shoulder and pressed the button on his radio. "Need backup in the nurse's office."

Edward had both hands around the neck of the officer named Jim. He seemed mildly amused by the squishiness, like those tube-shaped toys that slip out of your hands when you squeeze them. Every time he tightened his grip, the cop gave out a gurgle. Edward said, **"It's nice to feel things. He's got little bones in there."**

"Put him down, son," said Officer Tony — the one with the mustache and the gun. The barrel of his firearm was shaking in and out of a hit zone. Edward looked up. He seemed to notice Officer Tony's presence for the first time. The officer's command seemed to echo in the silence. The phrasing was unfortunate. Edward's perverse mind took it as an invitation. He shook Officer Jim with both hands, as if he were strangling a puppet. Then he slammed the officer's head into the examination table. The cop went limp. Edward smiled. Officer Tony took a step back into the wall.

Edward said, **"I don't feel the bones anymore."** He lifted the body in front of him and ran toward the door. All Officer Tony could see was his partner's back getting closer and closer. He made a startled grunt, then fired his gun. He aimed at the floor as a warning, but the bullet made a sharp *ping!* then ricocheted upward. A jar of cotton swabs on the back wall shattered.

Edward charged forward and shoved the limp body of the fallen officer into his partner as he ran out the door. As soon as Edward entered the hallway, he felt a sharp pain in the back of his head and crumbled to the floor.

⟫⟪

When Officer Tony stumbled out into the hallway, he saw Detective Mancuso standing over the young man, holstering his gun. Mancuso wasn't pleased.

"You fired your gun in a school?"

"He had Jimmy by the throat."

"In a friggin' rich school like this? They got SWAT on the way."

"Sorry. Let's book him."

Mancuso nodded. "Help me get him up."

The two men slapped the handcuffs on Edward just in time. As they dragged him out of the school, flailing and shouting like a wild animal, the students of Marlowe packed the hallways. As he passed Annie, Edward squinted, then smiled wickedly at her. She stared at the thuggish stranger as though she had met him someplace before. But before anyone could get a good look at him, the officers pulled him through the double doors and threw him into the back of their police van.

ANNIE'S CHOICE

I never thought you'd do it.

Well, I did.

I know. I just never thought you would.

OK.

Do you know how you got here?

Where?

With me in control. With you losing your own mind.

I took all the pills because the cop was gonna find me.

No. You took them because you finally figured it out.

Are you gonna say, 'It was inevitable'?

Wrong again. I was gonna say that you figured out that your mom—she's not here. Your dad—he's not here. You've been in a bad spot for weeks now, little boy, and nobody's noticed.

Wait. You think I tried to kill myself 'cause your mommy loves you more than my daddy loves me?

Don't be stupid, Tommy. You did kill yourself.

Annie watched the police drag the kid through the hall. She thought, *I've seen him before. I know I have.* But it was hard to get a good look. The cops got in the way as they wrestled the kid, who was thrashing around wildly. He tried to head-butt one of the officers but hit his shoulder instead. He pounded the shoulder several times, then tried to take a bite out of it. The officer groaned, then punched the kid in the gut.

"Kid" wasn't the right word. He looked like he should have been in college. His arms seemed too long. His head seemed too little.

Detective Mancuso, who wasn't in uniform, said something Annie couldn't hear. The cop jostled the kid some more and replied, "What? He friggin' tried to bite me."

Finally, they arrived at the double doors. The detective opened the one on the right, but the cop shoved the kid into the closed door by accident and ended up using his face to push it open. After a few noisy minutes, curious students began pouring out of the atrium. A girl named Lucy, standing near Annie, turned to a friend and said, "Ever since they started giving out scholarships, this place might as well be a public school."

"He didn't look like one of the urban kids," said her friend.

"Oh, Charlotte, don't be so racist. Anyone can be poor. My dad's sending me to Choate next year."

Annie gave them a sidelong glance and took a step away. Someone else in the crowd said, "Is that the guy who put Roger in a coma?"

Annie cringed at the name. The last time she had seen Roger was a few days ago. The hospital had moved him from intensive care to the main ward after the swelling had come down. For a while, they thought the trauma to his skull had caused brain damage, but when Roger woke up, he said, "I dreamed I went to Sea World — or was that real?"

Annie knew he was far from recovery. Maybe it was all the pain-killers. He slept nineteen hours a day, and when he was awake, he seemed distracted. Annie sat with him almost every day. As a joke she brought him a bunch of children's books. She'd read him the fairy tales and show him the pictures, as though he were five years old. Every once in a while, Roger would make a joke, but mostly he seemed apathetic and sleepy. Annie brought him a few trashy reality shows, but Roger wasn't up for the usual running commentary. Loud noises seemed to scare him. Any quick movement made him jump.

Annie knew that her best friend wasn't just going to get up from the hospital bed and pick up where they left off.

One night as Annie kissed him on the cheek and said good-bye, Roger asked, "They find him yet?" Annie shook her head. He sighed. "It was dark," he mumbled. "I didn't see him very well."

"They'll find him," she said.

"So he's out there, and I'm still in here. . . ." said Roger. He closed his eyes and turned his face into his pillow.

"I promise they'll find him," said Annie, feeling her cheeks flush.

"And then what? You'll beat him up for me?"

Annie paused. "No, I dunno. I'll make him send you an e-card."

Roger laughed. "Thanks, Annie. You're a good friend."

"A good *best* friend," said Annie.

Annie stood in the Marlowe hall, watching the same detective haul away Roger's attacker. Someone she knew from someplace, maybe a class freshman year. And her sometimes boyfriend, Thomas Goodman-Brown, was still nowhere to be seen. Annie wondered how much more F'd the situation could get. She was watching this and all she could think was how relieved she was that it wasn't Thomas.

Annie couldn't have articulated it until then — she couldn't bring herself to admit that, all this time, she had suspected Thomas. He had been acting so jittery, so torn up, that he must have been hiding something. The biggest piece of evidence — *was it even evidence?* — was the paper she had found in Marla's locker. The handwriting was definitely his. And if it wasn't evidence, it was certainly shady. It could have been a writing assignment, a persona poem. *Or maybe he was just cheating on me,* thought Annie with a bitter laugh. *Whatever it was, at least he wasn't —*

"Evil?"

Annie whirled around at the sound of a female voice. It was Nicola Vileroy, Thomas's stepmother, dressed in a beige Chanel blouse and a pencil skirt. Annie instinctively took a step back.

"I was gonna say 'guilty.'" The words were out before she could take the time to wonder how Thomas's stepmother could know her thoughts. Maybe she had said it aloud.

"Aren't they the same thing?" said Vileroy.

Annie didn't have an answer. Madame Vileroy smiled, as though on cue. Her blue and branded eye twinkled. Annie was almost certain now that she hadn't spoken out loud.

"H-h-how did you . . . ?" Annie stammered.

Madame Vileroy nodded at the double doors and said, "Young men like that make you wonder if there is such a thing as pure evil."

Annie looked at the doors as well, even though there was no one there anymore. The way Vileroy spoke seemed almost wistful. As crazy as that sounded, Annie could have sworn that she was amused by it all.

"I hope Thomas is all right," said Annie, searching for something to say.

Vileroy looked at her. "Hmm?"

"Thomas," said Annie. "I haven't seen him in all this craziness, and I hope he's OK."

"I'm sure he was around," said Vileroy.

Annie nodded. They were the only two people left in the hallway. She wondered what Thomas's stepmother wanted. Neither of them said anything. Annie had never seen Madame Vileroy behave this way. Granted, she'd seen her only a couple times, at the wedding and a party or two. She snuck glances at the patrician lady, so nearly perfect in her physical features. But now she seemed purposeless, lost.

She seemed to be sleepwalking. Annie needed an exit strategy. She turned to Madame Vileroy and said, "Well, it was nice seeing you."

Before Annie could make her getaway, Vileroy snapped out of her contemplative gaze and said, "That's why I'm here."

"I'm sorry?"

"Thomas. I came to see his therapist. He's been very unwell,

Annie." Annie didn't know how to react. It couldn't be *that* bad if Vileroy was telling her about it. "I'm telling you this because he has been very . . . focused on you lately."

Madame Vileroy seemed genuinely concerned. "I don't want you to get hurt."

"Uh, OK," said Annie. "I have to go to class now."

She had already gone down the road of suspecting Thomas. Now she had decided to trust him.

Madame Vileroy glanced down the hall in both directions. Then she leaned toward Annie and spoke in a conspiratorial whisper: "His therapist had him write a journal, and I think, well, he seems to be dealing with a lot of guilt."

Vileroy took Annie's hand. Her grip was icy, almost painful. Annie tried to pull away, but Vileroy held on until, finally, Annie looked her in the eye.

"Be careful, Annie," said Madame Vileroy. She pressed a thin stack of folded paper into Annie's hand, then turned abruptly and walked away. Her high heels rapped out a sound like a twenty-one-gun salute.

Annie waited for her to leave—and for the echoing to stop. "Weird," she said under her breath.

The way Madame Vileroy talked, it seemed as though she might be afraid of Thomas. Annie looked down at the pages. She recognized the handwriting—the same as the pages from Marla's locker. They were definitely from Thomas's journal. . . .

I asked her if she wanted to go skiing, and she said, "Sure, let me check with Roger," like he was her dad or something. Like she couldn't go take a walk in Central Park without his permission. . . .

Oh, and it wasn't "Roger"—it was "Rog" or "Roj" or however you spell it—she was like, "Let me ask . . . Roj."

What is that? Does she even know how that sounds? Wanna go out? I dunno, let me ask Roj. Want some hot sauce? I dunno, What Would Roj Do with HIS chicken platter?

I really like her, but I just get this feeling that the two of them are laughing about me all the time.

It continued for another page and a half. Annie was most unnerved by the fact that he never wrote her name. The handwriting became more and more erratic. Several pages later, it said:

I saw him at Elixir—I guess someone invited him and he didn't have to check with her first.

I followed him.

He saw me, but he didn't recognize me, 'cause I wasn't me.

He was with a friend, who asked him to keep him company while he grabbed a smoke out in the alley.

The friend stopped in the bathroom on their way. I pushed down a girl who got in my way. The guy's head hit the stall door—kept hitting the stall door till it cracked open.

Then the alley.

I went to see ol' Roj.

Annie gasped. The handwriting became jagged and illogical, but the image was clear. Only two people could have given such a detailed and horrific description of what had happened the night her best friend was attacked — Roger, and the monster who did it.

Annie's hand shook as she finished.

It was Thomas. He had beaten Roger to within an inch of his life. And whoever that was that the cops dragged away — *from the pancake social!* thought Annie; that was where she had seen him — that guy was Thomas's scapegoat. Paid off, or framed.

It was evil.

Annie walked to class in a daze. She'd made the wrong choice.

18

DOUBTING THOMAS

Saved Drafts

Dear Dad—

*I'm writing you through the in-game messaging sys-
tem 'cause my e-mail account is probably being monitored.
I figure Nicola doesn't pay much attention to a fantasy
RPG, so this is the best way to reach you. If you get this, it's
because I told one of our guildmates to log in to my account
if I'm not on for ten days and send you this message.*

*It means you're probably still out looking for me. Or, if
she's convinced you that I'm dead, I guess the funeral is over
and you're doing something like going through my things,
trying to figure out what went wrong.*

Well, I'll tell you: it was Vileroy.

*You brought her in, Dad. I always thought you'd give me
a little heads-up, but you didn't. For what it's worth, I'm not
mad about that anymore. I know what she can do, and even
if she didn't have supernatural powers of mind control, plus*

the French seduction skills, you still wouldn't owe me any-
thing. It's your life. I'm sorry about what I said about you
cheating on Mom. That one was a cheap shot.

I've lost track here. There's a lot to say, I guess, and I'm
in a hurry.

Dad, it was Nicola. She's not human. She's evil. I know
you won't believe me, so I made a case file. It's hidden in my
room in the place I hid Mom's things from Aunt Julie that
one time. Find it, Dad. It proves that I didn't run away or
kill myself.

I was murdered.

There's some strange stuff in there—I know. I know
how weird it sounds. But look at some of the facts, like how
she brainwashed the lady from Florida. . . . There's evidence.
I hope you see I'm still rational. In fact, I'm better than I've
been in a long time. I'm not obsessing over Belle anymore.

People will say I've gone crazy, especially Vileroy. But
you tell them that saying that is an ad hominem *attack,*
and it's not good debate. Show them my case. It's my best
work. I think I would have made a pretty good lawyer.
Anyway, I love you, Dad. This wasn't your fault.

Your son,

Thomas

"Get him in there, Detective. Get him in or I break his jaw," said
Officer Tony.

The two cops struggled to push Edward into the police van. Even with both hands cuffed behind his back, he had an unnatural strength. The officers each took an arm and shoved him toward the vehicle.

To make things worse, Edward was laughing at the sky like a madman. When he came to the van, he stepped onto the bumper and pushed backward as hard as he could. It caught both the cops by surprise. The back of Edward's head slammed into Officer Tony's nose. Blood splattered in every direction, as though the nose had been a giant mosquito.

Detective Mancuso took out his Taser and shoved the electric prongs into Edward's kidney. Even with fifty thousand volts flowing through him, Edward's howls were mixed with laughter.

"Do it again," he said.

Somewhere deep within Edward Hyde huddled the ghost of Thomas Goodman-Brown, overcome by the surge of W.

The detective sent another fifty thousand volts into Edward, then lifted him up by the elbow.

A crowd stood across the street. Some of them had their phones pointed at the scene. When he saw them, Mancuso put away his Taser and grabbed Edward by his back collar. Edward was panting, with his tongue hanging out. "You're a piece of trash," growled Mancuso. "I could have cooked you right here."

He lifted Edward, shoved him into the back of the van, and slammed the doors. Officer Tony was still crouched on the pavement, cupping his hands over his gushing nose.

216

Thomas opened his eyes. He was on the forward deck of a ship like the one from his semester at sea. The sails were full, tossing in the wind. The water was a deep orange, like blood without iron — an anemic ocean.

He knew somehow that he was meant to be here. It wasn't a dream his subconscious had fabricated. It *was* his subconscious, lost at sea.

⤛✦⤜

Edward landed on the metal floor of the police van in the dark. He smiled. His teeth were bloody. He could taste the iron on his tongue, but he couldn't tell if it was his blood or from one of the cops he had bitten. This body was still so new.

He hadn't heard Thomas's voice in a while. He couldn't feel him anymore, crowding the back of his mind. Maybe Richie Rich had finally died.

A voice interrupted.

"You put Jimmy in the hospital."

Edward looked up. Detective Mancuso sat on the bench along the wall of the SWAT-style vehicle. He didn't know Edward could see him in the dark. Mancuso looked like he was grinding his teeth.

"Is he the one I head-butted or the one I strangled?" said Edward.

"You broke half the bones in his neck," said Mancuso. He had something in his hand that glinted.

Edward sat up on his knees. **"You guys should give him a fun nickname to cheer him up, like Jimmy Two Clucks or Chicken Jim."**

Mancuso stayed silent. Edward could tell he was waiting for his eyes to adjust to the dark. "They're gonna take you to Police Plaza, and the first thing they'll do is take your mug shots. You know why?"

Edward leaned back on his knees and tried to bring his cuffed wrists under him. There wasn't enough room. He'd have to dislocate his own shoulders.

"So the news will have your face plastered online. But after you get your pictures taken, I'm gonna turn your face into mush. It'll be weeks before you gotta be in court . . . weeks before you gotta be pretty again."

Edward strained one more time. He planted his feet on the floor of the van, leaned back on the wall, and pressed as hard as he could, trying to get his hands — cuffed behind him — to reach his feet. It didn't work. As Mancuso continued to talk, he placed his fingers through the brass knuckles he was holding. "But for now, I'm thinking of playing xylophone on your ribs."

Edward let out a groan from straining himself. He said, **"You know, you really talk too much."**

Edward sprang from his haunches toward the detective and rammed his shoulder into the detective's chest. He could almost feel the air rush out of the detective's lungs. Edward fell on his back and laughed. Detective Mancuso doubled over him but couldn't do anything other than cough spittle all over Edward's face.

A storm rolled in and brought rain. The waves began to beat the side of the ship. The sails were being buffeted about. Thomas knew he should tie down the sails and get belowdeck before the hurricane really hit, but for some reason he couldn't remember how to do that. All the ropes and pulleys did something specific—he knew that much. He could remember a few of them, but not enough to accomplish anything. It was as though he had lost that part of himself. He looked down at his hands. The calluses he used to have from his time at sea were gone.

He couldn't concentrate here. He was cycling through so many emotions . . . first happy, then frustrated, then dazed, then homicidal. He couldn't control them, each pill, the individual pieces of Edward's soul, taking effect one by one.

When Thomas looked up, a dark figure stood in front of him. Thomas screamed. The figure was moving. It was made up of black creatures—insects, sea slime, little demonic things. They roiled in and around one another in the shape of a human. The form was nearly perfect—a female human, featureless except for an eye. The creatures avoided the eye. The empty space it made was in the shape of a cross. Everything else was as black as octopus ink.

Thomas shouted but the storm carried away the words. The figure stepped toward him. She reached for him with both arms, like a mother. Thomas recoiled. The insects moved as one hive, one Legion.

Thomas darted to the side just as the ship leaned into a wave. He almost stumbled into the figure, but he ducked and ran toward one of the life rafts on the side of the ship. Visibility was low because of the rain. The insects followed him.

He felt an out-of-place artificial sort of elation overcome him. He struggled not to surrender to it, not to lie there and dream when he should be fighting for his life.

A massive wave slammed into the ship and sent Thomas flying into the railing. His rib hit the bar so hard that he felt it crack.

⤳⤳⤳

"How's that feel?" said Detective Mancuso as he stomped on Edward's rib cage. "Feel good?"

Edward moaned, **"No."**

"Oh, yeah? What happened to the jokes, tough guy?" He stood over Edward, holding the handrails along the roof of the police van. Edward tried to roll over onto his stomach, but with his hands pinned under him, he couldn't get the leverage.

"What happened to 'You talk too much'? What happened to that?"

Mancuso lifted himself with the handrail and came down with both heels on Edward's sternum. "You think you can mouth off like that after putting a cop in the hospital? You think we just let punks like you get away with that?"

Mancuso began kicking Edward in the ribs. He couldn't get room in the van to really pull back, so he rapid-fired, kicking as hard as he could, over and over. As each rib began to break, Edward's moans turned into laughter. Mancuso kicked him one last time, and with that momentum, Edward finally rolled himself onto his stomach.

Mancuso was out of breath. The van took a right turn, probably onto Broadway. They would be at the station in ten minutes.

Edward mumbled something, but his face was toward the floor, so Mancuso didn't hear it.

"What'd you say?"

"I said 'xylophone.' You have a kid, don't you, Detective?"

220

Mancuso roared. He punched Edward in the kidneys with the brass knuckles. He grabbed the handcuffs and lifted Edward off the ground.

"Let me tell you something—"

But Edward didn't wait. He had what he needed. With a sudden lurch, he threw himself back down to the ground. Just as he planned, Mancuso held on to the handcuffs. His instinct was to hold on to the criminal. Mancuso heard two audible pops. Edward screamed in pain. Both his shoulders had been pulled out of their sockets.

Thomas reached into the chest with the life rafts and grabbed a wooden oar. The bloody waves poured over the ship. A crack of thunder resounded overhead. The figure reached Thomas and grabbed his shoulder. It felt like a thousand insects biting him at once. Thomas's shoulder was on fire.

Despite the pain, he felt himself vacillate between self-consciousness, dread, and euphoria. *This must be how he kills you,* he thought, wondering which emotion to believe.

He swung the oar with his other arm. It smacked into the side of the figure and continued through. When it emerged from the other side, the oar had been eaten away. Thomas pulled back. He knew it was Vileroy. The branded eye confirmed it.

This was her true form. She had invaded him, and with her son, she would make sure Thomas was dead.

Thomas shouted, "I know who you are!"

The figure continued toward him, expressionless.

"I know what you did to Belle and Bicé. I found them."

Even in the chaos of the storm, Thomas could see the change in the figure. The insects seemed to be agitated. The slimy black barnacles almost ground each other up.

"They beat you. And I know about the Darlings."

The figure surged at him, but Thomas evaded it just in time. He backpedaled around a mast and kept it between them.

"I know about the bonedust, Vileroy. I know W is your last hope."

The branded eye of the black figure seemed to flare with rage. Thomas took a step backward. In all the noise, he didn't hear the sail swinging across the ship toward him. The massive wooden boom hit him in the back of the head. The featureless face of Vileroy was the last thing he saw before blacking out.

Edward felt fireworks in his skull as he fell to the ground. Before Mancuso could grab him again, and before he blacked out from the pain, he quickly tucked his legs into his body and brought his arms under. He hands were in front of him. His arms were still incapacitated. They were cuffed, and his shoulders were dislocated.

Mancuso was panicked. He'd lost control of the situation. He cursed as he marched toward Edward and reached for him. This time, Edward stood up. He swung both his fists like dead weights and smashed the detective in the temple. Mancuso fell on the bench and hit his head again on the side of the van. His joints went limp as he lost consciousness.

Edward stood over the detective. The van took another turn,

banking to the left this time. Instead of catching himself, Edward used the momentum. He hurled himself at the side of the van, shoulder first.

He screamed when he made contact. A loud pop and the left shoulder jammed back into the socket.

Thomas jostled awake as fresh pain pierced his left shoulder. He must have fallen on it after the sail knocked him out. It had been the span of only a few seconds. The storm pelted him in the face. He saw the creatures called Madame Vileroy undulating as one hideous body.

She walked toward him. Thomas scrambled away, but the boat leaned once more toward her.

It seemed the storm, the rain, even the boat itself, was helping her. Thomas began to panic. He'd lost all control. He had —

Thomas looked out into the bottomless sea and realized why he was there. Why he was on a boat in the first place, when he could have been anywhere. Specifically, why he was on the same boat where he had mourned his mother. The place he'd given up.

The swarm grabbed at him, but Thomas had found new purpose. He turned toward the back of the ship and ran. Vileroy followed. Thomas dodged her pincers as he headed for the ship's tiller. He said to himself, "Steer the ship, Thomas. Steer the ship."

The full brunt of the storm crashed over the ship. Lightning webbed across the sky. Thomas slipped and nearly fell overboard. The insects hissed as they scurried toward him, but Thomas gained space by taking the stairs two at a time.

Suddenly he noticed something—a burgeoning confidence, his own genuine emotion winning out.

Just as he stepped onto the landing, he felt the mandibles of a dozen creatures bite into his ankle. Thomas cried out but kept going. He dove for the controls. He shouted, "It's mine now. The ship's mine."

He could almost feel Edward, somewhere nearby, take notice.

It's my ship now.

But Thomas had the helm now and he could feel the ship turn under his control, according to his will. He dared the next pill to take effect, to overcome him with feelings that were not his own. But the confidence of a moment ago only strengthened. Thomas knew this feeling. It was the elation of winning a debate tournament, of hitting a golf ball two strokes below par. This was Thomas's own true self.

Edward, it's time to die.

The Legion of insects towered over him, ready to strike. But Thomas was right. The storm let out a last crack of deafening thunder. The demoness disintegrated—like a crashing wave—and poured a thousand insects over the side of the ship.

With every ounce of consciousness he had left, Thomas summoned his body back, focusing every molecule of his physical self on banishing Edward.

Get out! Get out! Get out!

Thomas's chest heaved with relief and adrenaline. He had the ship.

Already, the ocean was calming. Thomas closed his eyes and let the gentle rocking motion bring him sleep.

⤛⤜

Thomas opened his eyes.

He was in a jostling van. The first thing he noticed was the undulating pain in his shoulders, his ribs, and his kidneys. The next was that he was handcuffed. He looked around. Detective Mancuso was unconscious at his feet.

Thomas didn't have much time. He knew where he was now. He remembered taking all the W, being lost in his own subconscious, then beating Edward for control. Now here he was, back in his own body. He felt his face and hair. He ached in the places he had been beaten, but his face was his own again—not Edward's but the face of an innocent bystander. Thankfully, his wrists weren't nearly as thick as Edward's. He squeezed his hands free of the cuffs. He checked the corners of the van to make sure there were no cameras, was certain not to touch anything with his own skinnier fingers, and waited for the van to stop at a red light.

Then he knocked open the door and fell into the street.

The light outside was blinding, but Thomas didn't have time to get used to it. He stumbled forward into the hood of a cab. "Hey!" said the cabbie. Thomas raised a hand in apology. He closed the van door just as the light turned green and let the cab pass.

He was downtown, near SoHo. Tourists and locals were meandering from shop to shop. No one noticed him. He was Thomas Goodman-Brown again. He'd be at school tomorrow, with a lot to explain to his friends—but also a lot of time to do it.

Edward had taken the guilt of all of Marlowe's crimes with him into oblivion. As for the police, they'd never see Edward Hyde again. No one would. He had lost. There was no more W to help him. Every piece of him was imprisoned in Thomas.

Thomas would never again surrender control. He'd proven that.

Thomas looked around the crowded city. He simply stepped onto the curb and walked uptown. He could have taken the subway, but his body ached. He didn't want to let anyone touch him. He just wanted to be alone for a while.

SCAPEGOAT

This morning something is missing. I feel cold, an impending doom, emptiness stretching out all the way into the future. It's a new sensation—the fear that there are no more long years ahead for me.

Edward is gone. My son is dead. Am I to die soon, too? I must prepare myself, because he was all I had left of my immortality. I must find a suitable place to die.

I stand in front of the mirror and stare at my face, the face I have built over millennia. I will miss it. I miss it each time I'm forced to take on the shape of the ugly old nursemaid or the mousy nurse or Nikki or any of the hundreds of others—none of these forms is my true self. My cheeks feel cold under my fingertips. Soon the flesh will be gone and I will be a vapor.

Maybe there is another chance. . . .

Maybe I can make one more grasp for a child—snatch one, just as I used to do in my younger days, right from under their noses.

Most of the time, people don't pay attention to what is right in front of them until it's far too late.

Fear gripped Thomas as he reached out to open the double doors leading into the Marlowe School. He took a deep breath. *Nobody knows it was me. Edward is gone and no one has any idea. Just be cool. . . .*

He pulled open the door and stepped into the long hallway. He winced from the pain in his shoulder. He hadn't gone to the hospital for fear of being caught, figuring that since his shoulders had snapped back into their sockets, they would heal on their own — and he had felt a little better each day, but he couldn't let on about the pain. The hall seemed strangely empty. Then he heard a chorus of laughs followed by hoots from across the corridor. He adjusted his backpack and started to make his way toward the noise. In the distance, he heard a girl giggle loudly and call someone a champ.

As he approached the far corner of the corridor, the noise grew louder. Boys cheering. Girls exclaiming. He even heard the voices of teachers mixed into the rabble. Around the corner, a crowd of kids and faculty were packed tightly around one locker — Roger's locker.

As he approached, Thomas caught sight of Roger standing in the center, the crowd mushrooming out around him and trailing back down the hall.

"What was it like?" said a freshman girl near the front. "Do you dream when you're in a coma?"

"Did it hurt?" said a girl in thick-rimmed glasses and a tattered faux-ho scarf. "What did the guy look like?"

Thomas felt his heart quicken, his feet frozen as he waited for Roger to respond.

"I don't remember much," he said. "It's like, yesterday I was here, and then I woke up, and now I'm here again. I don't remember the in-between stuff."

"You were very brave, Roger," said one of the teachers. "We're so glad to have you back."

A few of the younger kids clapped awkwardly, and from the back, Thomas could see that Roger was blushing, trying to get away from them. Annie was standing beside him. She was holding his arm and leaning toward him to whisper something.

"Yeah, but do you remember the guy who attacked you?" The question was coming from a sophomore boy that Thomas recognized as one of the writers for the school paper. He was carrying a notebook and scribbling things while sizing Roger up.

Roger looked flushed. He mumbled something, then said, a little quicker than normal, "They arrested the guy. He was big . . . that's all I remember."

The newspaper boy piped up again. "But you heard that he got away, right? Escaped right out of the back of the police van, so now he's out there, loose, probably dismembering or scalping something. . . . How does that make you feel?" He looked at Roger with big innocent eyes, as if he were asking about the weather.

A disapproving hum swept through the crowd. Connor Wirth, who was standing beside the newspaper kid, gave him a hard shove. "He *just* got back from the hospital. Give him a break, will you?"

"Sorry," said the young reporter. "Just curious."

Thomas studied Roger's face. He was wearing too much clothing, two sweaters stacked one over the other, as if he were cold all the time, even inside the school. He looked thinner, and there were still some bruises on his cheek. His right eye looked different, as if it had swollen and shrunk again and didn't quite match the rest of his face anymore. But more than anything else, the biggest change in Roger was the look of fear that colored his face as he looked cautiously from one classmate to the next. A surge of guilt swept over Thomas as he remembered that *he* had caused this. That it was his recklessness that had opened the door to Edward Hyde and to the permanent changes that had happened to Roger.

And what about Marla? The police still hadn't found her. Thomas had to do *something*.

He fought his way to the front of the crowd, trying to reach Annie. The teachers were starting to herd everyone away from the lockers and back to their classrooms, so it wasn't hard to meander through to where Annie was still clutching her best friend.

"Hey, Roger," Thomas said, a little awkwardly. He tried to tap him on the shoulder, but Roger moved away, probably from some newfound instinct.

"Sorry," said Thomas. He felt himself turning red, and he couldn't find anything appropriate to say.

"Nah," said Roger, "I'm just jumpy these days. What's up with you?"

"I'm glad you're back!" said Thomas, trying hard to sound cheerful. He turned to Annie. "Hey, let's take Roger out for a Frapp. First period's easy to skip anyway."

As he was waiting for her to answer, Thomas noticed for the first time that she wasn't so much looking at him as glaring. It was like she was trying to bore two eye-shaped holes into his forehead with the force of her death stare. When he smiled, she gazed angrily over his shoulder and played with a pencil in her hair.

"I'm going to world lit," she said, nervously crossing her arms. She took Roger's elbow and started to pull him in the direction of her English class.

"Hey," said Thomas. He moved along the row of lockers next to Annie and Roger. "What's going on? We're cool, right?"

"Cool? Are we *cool*? Hah!" She held more tightly to Roger's arm and looked at Thomas as if he were scum. "Come on, Roger."

Roger just followed along, even though it was obvious he wasn't exactly comfortable being dragged around like some kind of sick little brother. By the time Thomas could process what had just happened, Annie and Roger were halfway down the hall. Thomas slung his backpack over his shoulder and ran after them.

"Look, if you have something to say, say it." Out of habit, he found himself waiting for Edward to say something, to make a comment about how uptight she was, or how he would kill her. When the bad thoughts didn't come, Thomas smiled triumphantly, proud of having conquered the biggest demon he'd ever faced.

Unfortunately, the smile was just about the worst move he could have made in front of Annie.

"What's so funny?" said Annie. "Are you thinking about how much fun it was to beat up some poor kid just to get some cheap preppy-boy thrill? Do you find it funny? Well, I think you're disgusting."

Something caught in Thomas's chest — a tight feeling like each time he changed into Edward, like trying to swallow the whole bottle of pills and having them lodge just below his throat. He couldn't believe what he was hearing.

He looked around. There were a few students and some teachers left lingering in the hall. No one had heard.

"I didn't . . ." he began, but he didn't know how to finish. Did Annie think that he had attacked Roger? Did she know about Hyde?

"What are you talking about, Annie?" said Roger. "They arrested that other kid, remember? He's probably halfway to Montana by now."

"You know what?" said Annie. "I'm *glad* that kid got away from the cops. He was just a poor scapegoat anyway. Just some stooge you and your dad could buy off to take the blame for you. Real classy, Thomas." With that, she flung her books to the ground and stomped off, leaving Thomas and Roger staring dumbly at each other and at the pile of discarded homework scattering out from inside Annie's textbooks.

Thomas ran after her.

I can't believe this is happening.

He almost wished for a few of Edward's choice words right now, but once again felt a deep relief that no one else was commenting inside his head. It was just Thomas in there — alone, undisturbed. It was nice to have some privacy — some freedom — again.

"Annie, I don't know what you think you know, but I didn't do anything."

She stopped and turned, her ponytail flipping across her face.

"I read the journal, Thomas. I read every word. You attacked my friend. You hurt him and now he's . . . he's a different person."

Her eyes were filling with tears as she eyed Roger, who was lagging behind. Thomas wanted to try to hold her, make her feel better, but didn't dare get any closer. They both glanced back at Roger, lingering somewhere near his locker, unsure whether he should approach or let them talk alone.

Thomas whispered, "The guy they arrested . . . He's some juvie named Edward. I swear he's not a scapegoat. He's the one that did it, and now he's gotten away. We should focus on finding *him,* not on making random accusations." The words were coming out so fast that Thomas didn't stop to feel guilty for the awful lies spewing from his lips. Only when he paused to take a breath did the terrible feeling begin to overtake him. "Look, I'm sorry," he said, but she put up a hand.

"I know you did it," she said. "I can't believe how much crap people from this school get away with. I'm embarrassed to be a part of it." There was so much venom in her tone that Thomas didn't dare speak. He just turned over her words in his head and tried not to see the truth in them. She continued on, ignoring any sign of remorse or sadness that might have shown on his face. "Your dad either paid off the police and framed that poor kid or he paid the guy himself to take the fall. Either way, we both know *you* attacked Roger, don't we?"

Thomas began to answer, but before he could think of a good response, he realized something. Annie was right. He had always been saved by his father's name and fortune.

"How can I convince you?" he asked.

"Are you kidding me?" she shot back. "Why would I listen to anything you say? You're just lucky that I don't have the hard evidence or enough money to stand up to your dad. I tried telling that officer, but he said I was being paranoid, that this Edward kid did everything. But I swear, if I could prove it . . ."

For a second, Thomas wondered if he should tell her the truth. But he immediately dismissed the idea. The only way to prove to her that he was innocent would be to tell her about everything — the W, his stepmother's secrets, the supernatural things that had happened to him over the past few months. He couldn't do it. He realized now that Roger wasn't the only one who had changed. Thomas was different, too. From now on, and for the rest of his life, he would be more guarded, careful of everything he did and said, even afraid of the content of his thoughts. He would always be waiting for Edward to come back, or for his own strength of will to fail him. He didn't trust Annie enough to confess to her his most damning secrets.

Yes, Thomas Goodman-Brown was free now, to continue on with his life as Marlowe's resident golden boy. But Annie would never believe a word he said. And she would never forgive him. This would have to be the price of letting Hyde into his soul.

"Proof or no proof," said Annie, "I'm writing about this in the school paper. I'm telling everyone who will listen what I think really happened."

Thomas stared at his shoes. "I don't know what to say. . . . Stupid me. . . . For a minute, I thought we might still be friends."

Annie stared back at him, dumbfounded. "I never want to see you again."

20

ALONE AGAIN

"Edward? Edward, can you hear me out there?"

[Silence.]

"Edward? If you can hear, blow out this candle."

[Murmured incantations, a hiss, crackling flames, then silence.]

"Nicola? What are you doing in here? Are you . . . crying? I don't think I've ever seen you cry before."

"Oh, Charles. Sorry. I was just . . ."

"Muttering to yourself? Look, we need to talk. You saw the police sketch. I've met your son only once, but I have eyes, and we both know it was Edward who attacked those kids. You have to tell the police where he is."

"Please, dear, just leave me for now. . . ."

"What are you doing in here, anyway? Are those candles? And what is that awful smell? Are you burning something? Geez, Nic, you're creeping me out."

"Leave me alone, Charles!"

"You have to tell them where Edward went!"
"Edward is dead. He's dead."

With Edward's disappearance and the certainty that he was the criminal behind Roger's and Marla's cases, the police investigation was moved out of Marlowe. The commissioner put all his manpower on the task of finding the fugitive thug who had broken out of the police van and run off. The school was much quieter now, everyone having moved on to the next big Marlowe drama. Occasionally, Thomas overheard Principal Stevenson talking to the commissioner or one of the detectives about the status of the search, getting updates, probably passing them on to his assistant so that she could tailor soothing e-mails to the PTA. One morning Thomas was leaving his debate class when he saw Marla's mother, wearing all black, eyes full of tears, running out of the administrative office followed by a demure young woman, who Thomas guessed was her personal assistant, and a morose-looking middle-aged man, who could only have been Marla's father.

Everyone believed Marla was dead.

It made Thomas sick to his stomach. He couldn't get rid of the bad dreams or the awful pictures that ran all day in his head.

He was losing weight now, and one day as he passed by Roger and Annie, Roger stopped and said, "Wow, you're looking really off." Thomas smiled and walked on, knowing that he was pale and gaunt. Annie just glared. Suddenly, Thomas had an idea.

The journal.

Annie had read pages written by Hyde. Normally Thomas did not reread stuff in his notebook, but Edward had definitely written a few entries. Maybe there was a clue about Marla in his entries. Maybe she wasn't dead after all. Maybe she was still locked up somewhere, waiting to be rescued. Thomas was the only person who could save her, and maybe by doing so, he could save himself from a life of guilt and agony.

Sure, he would always have to look at Marla and Roger at school, or maybe later on in college or at parties. But at least he could live with what he had done if he knew he had tried to make it right. That he had saved Marla and that no one had died because of him.

Thomas grabbed on to the hope. Yes, maybe Marla was alive.

He brushed past Annie and Roger and ran toward the door, pulling out his cell to cancel all his activities for the day.

Thomas charged into his bedroom and grabbed his journal from his desk. It looked tattered, as if too many hands had touched it, too many fingers had flipped the pages. Some of the pages were torn out, and some were folded or cut in half. He wondered where the missing pages could be. The possibilities made him nervous, and he tried to calm down by remembering that he hadn't put his name anywhere on this book.

He began searching for clues.

An entry from the day after Marla disappeared seemed to go back and forth between himself and Hyde:

John says Marla disappeared right from her room. But I just saw her. Plus her house has security and there's a doorman. . . .

Maybe someone lured her out. . . .

Thomas stared at Hyde's words and rushed for his phone. He scrolled through his call history from the day Marla disappeared. Sure enough, there it was. He had called her, probably during one of his long blackouts. They hadn't been on the phone long, less than a minute. He checked his text messages. Nothing. Probably Hyde had deleted anything incriminating. But there was an outgoing message right after his call with Marla, to a number he didn't have in his contacts.

It said, *Same place as usual?*

Thomas sat down on his bed and took two deep breaths, thinking he would be sick right there on the floor. He clutched his phone tighter, considered calling the number again. He didn't. Instead, he went to his computer and entered the phone number in a few search engines. Probably nothing would come up. What criminal henchman would be dumb enough to have a listed number?

He was just about to give up when a single word in the Google results caught his eye. The number was next to a name: *Nikki*. Was this Nikki's number? The same Nikki who had given him the W in the first place? Could she be the one that Edward texted? He wished he had gotten Nikki's number at Elixir so he could compare it with this one. But then again, what was the point? Nikki had delivered the pills that turned him into Edward. She obviously worked for Nicola, just like Dr. Alma did. So it shouldn't be surprising that when Edward needed help kidnapping someone who knew a little too much, he would recruit Nikki to help him. Once again, the similarity in the two names struck him. What if Nicola *was* Nikki, the same way that Thomas was Edward? He pushed the thought out of his head.

Then another disturbing thought worked its way into his mind. The reason Marla had been kidnapped in the first place was that she knew about Roger. If he were to rescue her now, would she tell the cops? Had she seen Thomas in Edward's twisted face as he dragged her away to whatever psychotic torture room he had prepared? Edward had certainly used Thomas's phone, so Marla must have thought she was meeting Thomas that night.

Yes, Marla would know.

Yes, she would tell.

Still, Thomas knew he had to do this. He had to rescue Marla for the sake of his soul and sanity and because her life was more important than his freedom. Sure, he might get locked up. He might never grow up to do all the great things he had dreamed about. But he couldn't just let some girl die — not even an annoying goth girl.

He went back to his bed and picked up the journal, recapping to himself everything he now knew. Nikki had prepared a room. Edward had called Marla on Thomas's phone. He had lured her out somewhere.

Thomas flipped ahead a few pages to an entry from a week later.

Stupid modern goths. This chick doesn't even have a clue about the real thing. I showed her some pictures, real gruesome ones of attacks and battles — all blood and limbs. She couldn't handle it. Hah! I guess she just likes black hair dye and whiny music.

Hyde seemed to know a lot about Marla's interest in goth culture. It was starting to make sense, though. What else but something she was really interested in would cause a girl to sneak out to meet up with Thomas, a guy she hated, a guy that had just left her looking like a fool after a hookup? It had to be something she was really into. He remembered the poster in her room:

Samson Diablo: The Emo King of Spain

In concert ONE NIGHT ONLY @ Madison Square Garden

* Dress as your favorite goth character or pagan idol to be eligible for a door prize, courtesy of Diablo™ himself!

Then a vague memory, like a dream, began to take shape. These days he could never be sure which of the many Marla scenarios in his mind were real and which were just his imagination fueled by the fear of what he could have done. But this felt somehow different from the rest. He remembered thinking about that poster, talking to someone about it on the phone, then a laugh on the other end.

I didn't know you were into Diablo, Thomas!

I'm soooo into Diablo. Loved your poster.

Then fading laughter. Was it his laugh or hers? Maybe it was Edward's.

Back at his computer, Thomas looked up Samson Diablo. He found a list of appearances, concert photos, interviews with surprisingly Googleable "underground" goth publications. Then, as his cursor moved across the options, he saw that there was one link he had visited before. Strange. He didn't remember ever researching this douchy emo faux musician. The site was for an invitation-only meet and greet with Samson himself, scheduled for the same night that Marla was kidnapped.

⧫

The address for the meet and greet had been unfamiliar, but as Thomas strolled the smaller streets around it, he began to realize that he had been here before, and not just in some Hyde-induced blackout when he had no control of himself. He had been here in his regular life. Where was he exactly? He zoomed out the map on his phone.

It would make sense for Hyde to take Marla somewhere Thomas would know. But where would the meet and greet have taken place? There was nothing on this street but boarded-up stores and abandoned trash cans. The address was right, though. He took a few steps forward. Now he was standing in exactly the spot the website had advertised. But this was just some back alley.

He opened the website again. He noticed now that there were more than a hundred comments underneath.

Totally fake.

I never heard of this.

Diablo left town already. No way he's doing a private thing.

Every comment was about how the advertisement was a fake.

Thomas was about to close the page when he caught sight of the page administrator. Nik45666.

Figures. Nikki again. She must have made a fake website so that Marla would believe she was about to meet her idol.

He walked out of the alley and onto a bigger street, then onto an even bigger one with more traffic. He passed two men in suits coming home from work. Then a tired mother fumbling for her keys. Suddenly, it became painfully clear where he was.

He was standing right outside the Faust children's apartment.

"Yes, I'd like to leave an anonymous tip, please," said Thomas as he held the sleeve of his jacket over the mouthpiece of a well-hidden lobby phone in a random youth hostel in Midtown. This was probably far enough from the scene to ensure that he didn't get caught. It had been hard to find a public phone away from his usual hangouts, in a place with no passersby or attendants or video cameras. He had searched for more than an hour, thinking how hard it must have been for his dad when he was young and had to use these things every day.

"Name, please?" a nasal voice droned.

"Anonymous," Thomas snapped. Everything was so clear now. Edward would have used a place where he was a regular visitor — a place that belonged to him and his mother. A real Upper East Side prison. Thomas had seen enough mentions of dungeons in his journal to realize that it was the most likely place for Edward to use.

"How can I help you?" said the police station operator.

"I have a tip for Detective Mancuso. Please tell him that the missing girl Marla Harker is being held at this address." He paused, then added, "Actually, tell him there are *three* missing kids there. Tell him to dig around all the rooms. They're probably separated from one another, but there are definitely three."

He mumbled the address and quickly hung up, lowering his face as he left the hostel and rushed back home. If Marla *was* still alive, he probably had only a few hours to prepare before he would be dragged to prison for life. Still, despite the fact that he had almost gotten away with everything, despite having defeated Edward and escaped blame, he didn't regret his decision to risk it all again. It was well worth it.

<hr>

Thomas waited at home all night. He sat by his bed, his bags packed, looking at his sneakers and waiting for the officers to break in. Once in a while he turned on the TV to see if there was any news of Marla. He didn't dare call her house.

Packing had been an easy enough task. What could he take to jail? In the end, he grabbed only a book, thinking that it, too, would be taken away from him, but at least he could read during the long bouts of waiting while they booked him. He looked around his room and thought about how many expensive things he owned that he would never miss.

He wondered if he should say good-bye to his father.

Probably the cops would let him do that. And he would likely see his dad during the arraignment and trial. The whole thing would take a few months at least. . . .

There was a sharp knock on his door.

Thomas jumped, then clutched his chest and tried to breathe. He would have to learn to control these reactions or he would be eaten alive in jail.

"Come in," he said.

His father opened the door, face flushed, suit disheveled, and mumbled, "Hi, Son."

Thomas stood up and pulled his sack over his shoulder. "Don't say anything, Dad," he said, trying to hold back the tears. "I'm ready to go."

They stared at each other for a moment. Then his father said, "Where the hell are you going? I really can't deal with this now, Thomas."

Thomas opened his mouth. Then closed it. Then started to explain, when his father cut in. "Look, Son, I just wanted to tell you that they found your classmate Marla Harker. She's safe at home, so you can stop worrying. But I can't stay long because they need me at the lawyer's office. Apparently Nicola and I are *involved* now."

"Involved in what?" Thomas whispered through an almost-closed throat.

"We own some property that was used somehow. . . . Look, I have to run. I'm drowning in the fallout from this mess. But, please, don't pull some teenage runaway stunt tonight, OK? This family has been through enough. And things are not good with Nicola. Just sit tight until I get back."

His father glanced around Thomas's room, then looked his son in the face again, waiting for an answer. Thomas just nodded and forced a smile.

"Good," Mr. Goodman-Brown said, and began to hurry out.

"Dad, wait!" Thomas blurted.

Mr. Goodman-Brown stopped. "What is it?" he said, a little sharply.

244

"Is that all?" said Thomas, rubbing the back of his neck. It felt hot and wet. "I mean . . . did Marla say what happened?"

His father looked past Thomas and shook his head sadly. "Well, I suppose I should tell you so you know what to expect."

Thomas held his breath.

"Your friend Marla," said his father, "well, she was so drugged up, she could barely remember her own name. Nothing she says makes any sense. She probably won't be back at school for a while. And when she is, you and your friends should take it easy on her . . . with the questions and the gossip, I mean."

"What do you mean?" said Thomas, sitting down on his bed again.

"Apparently the first thing she did once she got home was to throw out all that goth stuff. She's probably just eager to start fresh, like all of us. . . . Oh, and you won't believe this, but they found some other kids, too. Bizarre."

Thomas raised an eyebrow. "So no sign of the kidnapper, then?"

Mr. Goodman-Brown cleared his throat. "Look, Thomas, just one other thing. You won't be seeing your stepbrother, Edward, anymore. He's trouble, and you're never to mention him to anyone, OK?"

DIVORCE ANNOUNCEMENT

Charles Goodman-Brown, financier and head of one of New York's largest financial institutions, and his wife, the governess Nicola Vileroy, announced their separation, followed by a quick divorce last week. The pair has not been seen in public together for some time, and it is rumored that Ms. Vileroy has moved back to her home country of France.

— C'est la Vie, NYC gossip blog

She stands in front of the mirror, touching her face, running her fingers across her many bottles and powders. It is happening at a frightful speed. She watches as the decades, the centuries, and the millennia appear and disappear in the mirror like flashes in a cauldron. Her heart quickens, then dies down again like a spent motor.

She is dying.

Today is her last day, because Edward, her immortal soul, is gone.

Her face is changing by the half hour, slow enough that she can mourn, but still far too fast. It is a punishment, a slow torture, watching herself deteriorate and waste away. She remembers her days as a girl in Egypt, millennia ago, when she was human and had the mundane dreams of small children.

Deep in thought, she almost misses the last of the beautiful blond governess. Within minutes, that face is gone and she is only the mousy nurse. How strangely similar they are. What separated the two but a few lines on her face, a few inches of height, a deeper tan here, a darker color there.

Now even the plain-faced nurse is gone. Now she sees another face emerging. The face of pure hatred and malice that lies beneath it all. The old hag. The nanny with the hunched back and the winding and deep caverns chiseled in her face. There is no point anymore in taking inventory. All the life she had built and stored up in jars and pills and potions is gone.

She is so very ugly now. She rests her face on the table and takes two shallow breaths, letting the moths hover over her lifeless head with its tangle of gray matted hair, like a nest of snakes, long dead in a pit.

Soon there is nothing left but a lingering murk. A dark cloud of half-formed insects, dust, sickness, and death. The shape of the woman begins to dissipate, wafting toward the window.

And finally, finally, the blue and branded eye flickers, then fades into nothing.

———

After cross-referencing the primary texts from the Egyptian scrolls (including secondary evidence from the Book of Gates*), eastern European fables about the "one-eyed witch," and historical accounts in England (regarding both the demoness and her son), we can* conclude that the demon Vileroy was one of the longest-lived demons. In total she may have captured thousands of unsuspecting souls. The ripples she produced undoubtedly ruined millions. She was a Legion on her own and might have corrupted so many more had she not let her life source be depleted, had she not underestimated the strength of humans. That was her weakness. . . .

As I have tried to establish in this thesis on demonology, our decisions follow us into the afterlife, and even there, the angels and demons have their own to make. Nicola Vileroy nearly accomplished immortality, but she fell just short and was forever destroyed.

It is fitting, then, to end with a quote from a mythic text, the Book of Legion, regarding demon eulogies: "We will not honor them for their conquests when they are gone, and we will not strain to remember their accomplishments, because that is not the work we do."

—*from* Demon Histories, *by Jamie West*
(born Christian Faust), Professor of Humanities